CLACKAMAS LITERARY REVIEW

2019
Volume XXIII

Clackamas Community College
Oregon City, Oregon

CLR
CLACKAMAS LITERARY REVIEW

Managing Editor
Matthew Warren

Associate Editors

Jennifer Davis	Ryan Davis	Trevor Dodge
Jack Eikrem	Delilah Martinez	Nicole Rosevear
Robert Shaffer	Amy Warren	

Assistant Editors & Designers

Kehau Aipolani	Eden Bell	Hannah Burley
Hannah Davis	Judith DeVilliers	Elias M. Eshelman
Katie Evans	Edan James-Wadsworth	Nathaniel Klein
Jeff Lowry	Ali Noman	Jordan Runyen
	Alicia Schmidt	

Cover Art
Do You Dream? by Katie Evans

The *Clackamas Literary Review* is published annually at Clackamas Community College. Manuscripts are read from September 1st to December 31st. By submitting your work to *CLR*, you indicate your consent for us to publish accepted work in print and online. Issues I–XI are available through our website; issues XII–XXII are available on our Submittable, and through your favorite online bookseller.

Clackamas Literary Review
19600 Molalla Avenue, Oregon City, Oregon 97045
ISBN: 978-1-7320333-1-3
Printed by Lightning Source
www.clackamasliteraryreview.org

Acknowledgments

Special thanks to Literary Arts for awarding the *Clackamas Literary Review* its 2018 Oregon Literary Fellowship for Publishers. We could not be more grateful for Literary Art's support and leadership.

And special thanks to Ooligan Press and the Write to Publish writing contest for partnering with our magazine to publish its 2019 poetry award recipient. We're proud to be part of this amazing opportunity and experience for writers and poets.

CONTENTS

EDITORS' NOTE

POETRY

John Sibley Williams	Genesis	1
Chad Bartlett	Liebestraum	2
Ace Boggess	"What Syllable Do I Chant for God to Hear Me, and at What Frequency?"	3
Douglas Cole	Fall	16
Nancy Flynn	Lowndes County, Alabama	17
Tim Gillespie	The Old Men of Argos	18
Larry Beckett	Madrigals	20
Diane Averill	Circe: My Story	22
Cecil Morris	Transubstantiation	24
Peter Serchuk	This Just In	26
Chelsea Thiel	Death Keeps a Garden	39
Marie Hartung	The Real Truth about Winter	40
Tim Gillespie	Dirtwork: The Spring Campaign	42
Matthew J. Spireng	A Horse in Custer's Column Survives at Little Bighorn	44
Simon Anton Niño Baena	Austerity	46
Francis Opila	The Picnic	48
Marie Hartung	It Could Have Turned Out Different in a Different Story	58
Mark Rubin	Poetry and Sex	60

Taylor Gaede	Unruly	62
Christine DeSimone	My Best Friend's Secret	70
Mark Rubin	My Her/Him Hirman	72
Taylor Gaede	You Are Not Who You Are	74
Marie Hartung	Quadratic	76
Madronna Holden	If You Could Tell Your Story with Wings	87
Nancy Flynn	One June Day: Fire, Heat, and Children Locked in Cages at the Texas-Mexico Border	89
John Sibley Williams	Straw, Sticks, & Brick	91
Christine DeSimone	Zum Wohl	93
Diane Averill	Where Lovers Meet	104
Peter Serchuk	The Man Who Cuts My Hair	106
Tara K. Shepersky	A Question of Time	108
Matthew J. Spireng	Strangers	110
Christine DeSimone	In Order	125
James Croal Jackson	A.S.	127
Jeffrey Alfier	Sketch of a Winnemucca Summer Night	128
Corey S. Pressman	Decay	133
Nick Conrad	February, a Roadside Sumac	134
Suzy Harris	What Is Possible	135
Jesse Gardner	The Rhythms of the Write	137
Chad Bartlett	San Simeon	153
Jeffrey Alfier	Breaking with Still Life at the Ranch Motel, Opelousas, Louisiana	154
Chelsea Thiel	The Dark Inside	155

Linda Neal	Perpetual Summer	160
Mark Rubin	The Cure for Acne	162
Chelsea Thiel	Unsavory	172
Holly Day	A House for Tiny Spirits	173
Suzy Harris	Learning to Hear Again	177
John Sibley Williams	Just Like This	179
Tim Gillespie	Cassandra in Three Acts	180
Madronna Holden	Advice from the Oregon Iris	183

PROSE

Daniel J. Nickolas	A Gallery	5
Ty Phelps	What They Did When the Moon Died	27
Will Radke	Waiting Stops	50
David Mihalyov	Beirut	63
LaVonne Griffin-Valade	Eureka	111
John P. Kristofco	No Man's Land	129
Will Donnelly	Even When We Are Not Ready	139
Jeffrey S. Chapman	The Card-Counter	156
Evan Morgan Williams	The Hiding Place	164
Ben Slotky	You're Not Wrong Forever	174

POSSIBILITY

Susan Bruns Rowe	Executive Order: Jerome County, Idaho	79
Hollyn Taylor	Mud	95

CONTRIBUTORS 187

Editors' Note

Few things bridge distance quite like the written word. Writing can carry ideas beyond cultures, generations, and borders. For writers, those impossible optimists, this journey involves ideas too stubborn to relinquish, shaped by long nights before page or screen—smudged ink, sweaty keystrokes, picky edits, fleeting inspiration, quiet doubts, and even quieter resolve—all to get ideas out to the world.

Some of these writers' ideas have made their way to us, the editors of *Clackamas Literary Review*. For the past several months we have come together to read and re-read, discuss, debate, and wrestle through each submission, spending hours dissecting pieces we were unsure about and fighting for the stories and poems we loved. Our discussions stirred deeper thought, challenging us in unexpected ways as we reconciled differing perspectives. Often this allowed us to see things in a new light, as beloved pieces were turned away and ones we did not first appreciate became favorites. Slowly, something that began as many individual efforts became a collaborative experience, reminding us that dissonance and diversity are part of a written work's journey.

In this world that feels increasingly disconnected and isolated, each piece you are about to read was created by a soul seeking connection. A connection to someone like you. Countless hours have been spent in service of the book you now hold in your hands and the connections it creates. Enjoy the variety of works in this volume; let them sink in and become part of who you are—part of *your* journey through the messy, chaotic, wonderful world we live in. And may the experience lead you to find something new of yourself along the way.

Genesis

John Sibley Williams

That in the beginning nothing was
known of the beginning only explains
so much. That our fathers had fathers
who traced their trembling back
to strange sources. Rain as weeping.
Storm: rage. All the suffering
wrapped up in us: deserved. & the awe,
the rinds of light that make their way
down here, burning like an anthem.

When the sky can't fill it all in, I too
color outside the edges. Isn't that what
edges are for? Like rules, how they say
you must master before breaking them.
Like how the field is only filled with
what we can see in the field. Doe tracks.
Wolf tracks. Waiting. So much waiting for
our turn. Everything burning endlessly
with the odor of its birth.

Liebestraum

Chad Bartlett

The moon tonight flutters when I touch it
like a decade-long dream in which I
have found the music that opens everything.

Cellos vibrate low tones, radiating gray
dust circles around us, bows dragged slowly
to prolong notes' long decay. No silence

here, but perpetual loss. The moon now burns
away like old celluloid, the only print of
a silent film disintegrating, hum of strings

fading.

"What Syllable Do I Chant for God to Hear Me, and at What Frequency?"

Question asked by Karen Craigo

Ace Boggess

It plays in B-flat, the same resonating, omnipresent,
from radiators, power lines, low thrum of machinery.
How it throats its solo sutra, *sotto voce*, always
though we've tuned it out, absolving our ears of its static
like an echo left from the Big Bang: not Zen *Om*,
but *Oh* of a sigh—pleasant release, fracture of self.
It moans in harmony with us to recognize
our hard luck, stubbed toes, existential doubts.
It sings along to sudden hymns of gratitude
when good news or friends arrive.
Oh, we whisper, squinting, as confusion handcuffs us
or a hiccough catches us unguarded. *Oh*,
we bellow at the brightening of enlightenment.
Buber preferred to speak '*Thou*' because
in that word we address the god in us,
god in one another, god in God, but no,
it's *Oh*, the simplest & most common.
It comes, precedes '*Lord*' in pleading,
'*yes*' in ecstasy. *Oh*, we mutter when we learn
the answer to a question that confounded us.

"What Syllable Do I Chant for God to Hear Me, and at What Frequency?"

Oh, we gasp when we don't find out.
We love that universal tone: a lyrical B-flat
conceived at the backs of our tongues,
nearer our hearts than our sexes or brains,
divinity nesting at the B-flat center of being.

A Gallery

Daniel J. Nickolas

Painting One:

The painting that hung in the sun-struck lobby of the Crestview Community College auditorium was a colossus, yet inattentive passersby mistook it for a simple change of pattern on the wall. The texture and style of the painting was done with great care and skill by a committed hand, deft and well trained. A boy named Tyler, who possessed the clever-cute demeanor of a raccoon, stood waiting for a theater class to begin. A friend of his, named Rebecca, stood with him.

"It's not really black and white, is it? Rebecca asked her friend. Her eyes fluttered like a dragonfly from one side of the painting to the other, trying to take in the image as a whole. The painting evoked a valley tree in misty midwinter, seen just as the soon-dawning sun turns the horizon cobalt and grey. "Wait, no. It's just a trick of the light, isn't it? I thought there was color in it, but it's just a glare from the sun."

"There's a lot of color in it." Tyler said, rummaging through the image's subtle details that proved him right. "The outline on the tree's stump has color, and the sky fades from white, to grey, to dark blue, not black."

"It's strange." Rebecca reexamined the painting, waiting for clarity to dispel the mystery. Nothing came to her. "I heard that a student painted this, but I don't know if I believe that. Why wouldn't the school get something done by a professional? Especially something that's hung where everyone can see it."

"Financial thing, maybe?"

"I guess. It seems like a professional might donate their work to a school—get some exposure in the process. Nobody gets anything with a student painting." Rebecca's posture straightened; a counter melody had begun over the conversation, a percussive click that was precise, solid, and consistent.

Professor Lapis stopped next to Tyler and Rebecca and the painting. Now still, her high heels no longer echoed the sweet *tap-click* through the cavernous lobby. "You two are early for class." She winked. From her earrings, genuine bluejay feathers dangled.

Rebecca's attention was still given to the painting; she acknowledged her teacher's presence only as a means to clarify her own curiosity. "Professor Lapis, do you know who painted this? I heard it was a student, but I wasn't sure that was true."

Professor Lapis let out an alto laugh. "There's a name plaque right next to the painting, here." She took a few steps to where the canvass ended, and indicated a small plaque with title, date created, and 'student-artist' name all in silver on oak. "If you're going to be observant, be observant." Professor Lapis turned and began to walk away. "And don't be late." The clicking of her heels dissipated into the auditorium.

Tyler watched his teacher, curious. "I can't figure out if Professor Lapis is really smart, or just passively mean."

Rebecca scanned the plaque. "I know this guy. Or at least I think I do."

"Who is he?" Tyler stood facing the entryway to the auditorium.

"He has American History with me. And I usually see him in the lunchroom after Method class." (Theater 203: Method Acting with

A Gallery

Prof. Lapis). Rebecca pulled gently on a lock of her hair. "I wouldn't have guessed he had such an artistic fire in him. We should go meet him."

"That one guy from history class becomes suddenly attractive, eh?" He put a hand on the small of Rebecca's back as a means of guiding her into class.

"That's not it at all."

Like any wandering minds, Tyler and Rebecca would have forgotten about the painting and its creator, except that a person cannot leave the auditorium without becoming the painting's audience. This is especially true for people heading to the cafeteria, the place Tyler and Rebecca always went after Method class.

The "cafeteria" was two separate rooms, normally divided by an accordion wall, which blurred together between 10:30 a.m. and 2:45 p.m. The second room, the one without an attached kitchen, was a large open grey space which, depending on time of day, was used for studying, socializing, or eating. Most student artwork was displayed here among the great throng of young, intellectually hungry minds—the place it was most likely to be ignored. The area smelled of franchised coffee and mock Italian food kept warm under heat lamps. The economy carpet hosted a number of captivating stain patterns; if a person looked hard enough they could find images, like with clouds. The marks left by blackberry cobblers were the most entrancing.

"There he is." Rebecca pointed out the artist of the lobby piece. He sat in a plastic, teal chair and read an art history book in a far corner.

"He's kind of bizarre looking." Tyler was unable to see the face behind the textbook.

Rebecca shushed her friend with an inane fear that the artist might hear him.

Tyler, having achieved the desired reaction from Rebecca, went on. "I'm just saying. I admit he's talented, but I don't know if that makes up for the Norman Bates post *Psycho* vibe I'm getting."

"What are you even talking about?"

Tyler smiled wide. "Sorry. I was only trying to help because I thought you might be love-blinded by your attraction to his artistic fire."

"You're so difficult sometimes."

For a moment, Tyler forcibly subdued his laughter, like a thumb on a champagne cork after the wire seal is removed. Once the need to tease passed, he sighed and became bored. "I don't understand why you care. I get that you're not actually attracted to him, so what is it? Do you want to be friends with him?"

The question struck Rebecca. "Well, no. I've never even talked to him before. I just thought it was interesting. I didn't know he was a painter."

"*Okay.* Do you want to go over and introduce yourself or something?"

"I don't know. Should we? He is alone."

"This isn't high school Rebecca; people eat alone because they want to be alone. Anyway, I'm hungry. Let's get sandwiches?"

"Maybe." She continued looking at the artist in the chair. She heard Tyler say something about saving her a place in the lunch line, then felt his presence dart away from her. She became self-conscious of the fact that now she was alone, standing and staring. The artist glanced up from his book, and looked at her. Rebecca turned her eyes away. She decided to follow after Tyler. From the lunch line, she could see the artist as he stood and walked across the room with a stride of purpose, as though he had somewhere to go. Tyler had been right, she thought. Rebecca wouldn't have considered it further, except that after she and Tyler finished their lunches, she saw the artist, out of the corner of her eye, again sitting in the plastic, teal chair.

Painting Two:
"He comes in every week to look at paints for about thirty minutes and buys whatever catches his fancy. Then he leaves." Mary Hanger of Hanger Arts Emporium speaks to her friend Carrie. She speaks about a man who is coming through the door. "By himself as always. And I can't imagine he uses all the paint that he buys."

The operatic coloratura Joan Sutherland sings a soaring E-flat over the sound system.

"Certainly handsome enough to have a fiancée or serious girl-friend." Carrie says. Carrie is a woman with heavy makeup and a heavier bundle of coats to protect her rheumatic body from the winter cold outside. A wind gust rattles the window and rustles the leaves of the tree by the store front. "He does have an intensity about him, doesn't he?" Carrie leans against the checkout counter, peers over her shoulder, and watches the man.

The artist about whom the women gossip is peculiar about buying paints. He picks five or six color swatches and arranges them in different patterns. In the first experiment, each swatch is different. In the next, he takes five swatches of one color and a sixth of a different color to see how the one looks when surrounded. He scrutinizes each paint brush by twisting the handle with his thumb and middle finger, but examines the bristles with his eyes only.

"He kind of makes me sad, I think." Mary says as Joan Sutherland's E-flat continues to ring irreverently against all other notes. There is too much of this music for Mary to be sad.

Carrie peers at her friend. "Why?"

"I don't know. He always comes on Saturdays. He never says a word except 'excuse me'; he gets so absorbed in the swatches that he sometimes runs into other customers." With her fingers, Mary combs her hair, dyed black as the stem of Maidenhair ferns.

"What does he say when he comes to the register to buy his paint?" Carrie's wrinkled fingers comb her hair of cornflower dust.

"I don't know. 'Just these today' or something like that."

"Don't you ever say anything back?"

"*My* job is not only to sell art supplies, but to recognize when customers aren't in the mood to talk."

"Still, if he really is here every week like you say, I'd expect you would've struck up a conversation or two with him by now."

"I think about it sometimes." Mary bats innocent eyes. "But he never strikes me as being in the mood for small talk." Mary watches the man as he carefully puts each color swatch back in its rightful slot. Mary respects him for it. The man goes over to the tubes of paint and picks those that correspond to the preferred swatches.

"Here he comes." Carrie inflects the sentence upward, and holds the "m" for a few seconds. "And I have some errands to run. Call me after you close." Carrie buttons her coat against the cold, and hobbles outside into the winter mist.

"Hello again." Mary says smiling. It is the same obligatory smile she offers to all customers, but she hopes it will mean more this time.

In a double fist, the customer raises his collection of items to the counter. "I'm taking only these today." A brief chaos ensues as he sets the items down.

Mary begins scanning the tubes of paint. Artic Oceans and the German Iris are first. Is she scanning to the rhythm of the Sutherland song? Mary must be quite musical and "You must be quite the painter."

"Yeah, you can say that."

"Do you paint professionally?"

"I haven't quite my day job." His expression indicates some awareness of a misstep; he pulls his grin and gaze to the ground.

She laughs. "What do you paint?" Neptune and several Moonless Midnights are passing over the price checker.

"Whatever I think to paint. I paint things that are grey, but I try to incorporate color into the greyness, as much as I can. I want people to see the color only after they look closely at the painting. I want them, at first, to see it in black and white."

"That explains these." A single Plumb is followed by a handful of Charcoal, Chalk, and a jumbo sized Onyx. Laughing, she expects him to smile at her observation. He does, but it is not the smile she wants. She is frustrated, though her effort costs her nothing. "That's a neat idea anyway." She puts the paint tubes into a plastic bag with her surname stamped across the front.

"Thank you." He takes the bag. "I need all these for a new piece I'm starting. I'm going to try something different."

Mary is silent. She hopes he'll elaborate. Her customer ties the handles of the bag into a knot so nothing escapes, says *thank you* and *goodbye*, and walks out of the store. Joan Sutherland's E-flat continues to ring with joy. But the song ends as the door shuts.

Later this evening, Mary will call Carrie as promised. Eventually the subject of the customer will come up and Carrie will be anxious to know about him. Mary will recount all she can remember. She'll end the topic by explaining to Carrie that the customer really is a person who just doesn't care for small talk, but that she gave him a free tube of Summer Limes as a gesture of goodwill.

"That was an empty gesture." Carrie will say.

Painting Three:
There was a general stride among the hired collective of wait staff who maneuvered around the flow of buyers, critics, and admirers. One member of the collective darted over to take empty bottles away from the wine bar, while another placed red stickers on the wall to indicate an item as sold. The Artist on display found himself apprehensive about the exhibition. Most of these paintings had already been seen by the public in other galleries, and the Artist-of-the-Hour had experienced too many rejections over the years to still be concerned for the opinion of strangers now. There was one thing, however, that worried him.

"What do you think about it, Timothy?"

Timothy, the Artist's agent, looked over as though he hadn't realized anyone was standing next to him. "What about?"

The Artist opened his mouth to repeat the question, but hesitated. "What do you think about the new work?"

Timothy chuckled. "Your tie is all wrong." He reached over to straighten the bow tie his artist wore. "I wish you could've finished painting number three in time for this showing. Numbers one and two are excellent, but I doubt they'll sell as an incomplete set." Timothy referred to the Artist's most recent endeavor called *The Blue Set*. "I had a feeling you wouldn't finish before tonight, and once again I've proven that I know you too well. Plus your intention for that piece, trying to make—how did you phrase it—'make blue catch fire.' It sounds like an impossible undertaking. Blue is a cold color, you know." Timothy finished with the bow tie, and after brushing a flake of dust from the Artist's cerulean button up shirt, was satisfied.

"You mean a *cool* color. Blue is a cool color. But there is this fervid intensity behind it; that's what fascinates me so much about it." As he spoke, The Artist's eyes narrowed while his cupped hands bounced gently in front of him as if to catch and order his words. "That's what I wanted to convey in these new pieces."

Timothy waved a hand and spoke playfully. "No, I get it. And of course I like your work, but what do you really care what I think? I'm just the guy who gets everybody as obsessed about your work as you are. You're talented, but I'm the people person. That's what makes us a good team." He laughed, and placing a firm hand on the Artist's shoulder asked, "How about some wine buddy? You seem on edge."

The Artist turned his head away from Timothy. "You don't have any opinion on it?" He looked at painting number two of the set, and appeared to talk to no one at all. Number two was the last transitional piece; he had accomplished the intent of his work in number three. Everything preceding number three was now part of the past. And there was number two, a ghost forever residing in a single passing moment, a visitant stuck on the threshold between realities. It was the spark fringed by glass powder and white phosphorus.

Timothy placed his other hand on the Artist's other shoulder. He spoke frankly. "I understand you're nervous about the gallery showing, but just keep it together; it will all be fine. It always is." The Artist continued to gaze at the specter and its colors of smoke from kindling about to ignite. Tim continued. "Anyway, this catering company doesn't always pick out stellar red wines, but the Shiraz is good. Let me get you a glass?"

The aura that held the Artist's attention must have left at that moment, because his eyes broke their focus from the painting and now looked down to Timothy's shoes. The Artist noticed that Tim's socks didn't match. The color of one was so close to the color of the other that only in gallery light, designed to emphasize the uniqueness of each shade and hue, could the difference be so clearly seen. "No thank you Tim. I'm not nervous."

"I'm glad to hear it. This is going to be a good night for you buddy." Deciding on a glass of wine for himself, Timothy turned and left.

"I just thought you'd have an opinion." The Artist said to open space. He agreed with Timothy. He too wished the third painting of the set could be present.

The gallery show ended. The Artist went back to his apartment and the empty tubes of paint, which he often let pile up into a mound before finally recycling them. The gallery showing was a success, as much as could be expected. He'd sold six paintings, and had two more commissioned by a semi-famous restaurateur.

The Artist loomed over the large fireplace in his living room, a brick chamber acting as an alternative to central heating. The room was cold, so he made a fire. He watched the kindling wood nurse the match's infant spark into a mature flame. "Difficult." He said to the fire. "I try not to be, but I am difficult." It wasn't the first time he'd been upset with himself for mistaking a professional relationship for one of friendship, but Timothy had been more convincing in the latter role than anyone before. But who was Timothy? The Artist had attempted to know, but still did not know. And he was unknown by Tim.

At the fire's core, he spied a blue flame, sudden and stark, but fleeting. He smiled, and placed a log in the fire. The words were nearly mouthed, but managed to escape on a whisper, "I keep missing you little flame."

The Artist walked over to the other side of the living room, where a sheet hung over a large rectangle leaning against the wall. He pulled the sheet off. The object was a canvas, number three from the set. He ran his hand softly down the dried paint. There was a sense of surrealism about the existence of the painting, a disbelief that it was really his. It was his style, his technique, his voice—his voice perfected. He remembered the countless hours he'd spent on it; he remembered every tube, and brush, and trip to the sink to empty and replace the water from the cleaning jar. He couldn't admit to Timothy that it was finished. He couldn't admit it to anyone, until there was someone to admit it to. "I think, I am too difficult."

His hand reached the point where it could brush down no farther. He moved it back up the painting, careful to remain as gentle as before. "I am too difficult." From the toolbox he retrieved a pen knife used to cut excess canvas from a frame. Guided by his hand, the knife ran a slit down the center of the painting, and then cut across the top and bottom so the canvas opened like a set of French doors. From the doors, he cut strips, one at a time. Whenever he saw a flicker of blue in the fire, he'd toss a strip into the heat, again and again until nothing remained.

Fall

Douglas Cole

nothing is official nothing but a cold day
nothing and nothing is holding us up
even as she shimmers behind her secrecy
you see there is a universal frequency we ride
like servers in and out of dining rooms
arriving unannounced except for disturbed air
and her hair goes golden white like waves
crest-breaking on the Sound out there
in turbulent and constant fragmentation
reassembling at last like magic
but nothing is magic or escaping your view
and nothing is taking your coat
when you come in from the cold
and fall into bed and rise again renewed

Lowndes County, Alabama

Nancy Flynn

There is no rest for the work of worms.
This land of the lost gray bleats to the beat of a crow.
Away from sleep where coffee breaks a molasses fog.
My morning tongue grieves the benighted and dismissed.

What faulty ways I find to speak, to navigate.
Such sighs of hurt.
Unsettled by lash, unleashed by the funk of neglect.
A life might be saved by a halo of mercies, or grace.

But here, on earth, a backhoe is needed to scrape aside the gone.
No stars, all bars.
Magnolias flower as flags snap, ordered to occupy their posts.
Once upon.

This time.
Poverty is a bullet-holed pane, a trailer askew on its particleboard base.
A grave is a muddy, hook-wormed ditch.
There is no rest for the worn, the worked.

The Old Men of Argos

Tim Gillespie

The old men of Argos,
warriors no more
(left behind when the Greeks,
puffed up, sailed to Troy,
their thousand-craft armada
packed with an army
of armor clad men-boys),
stood slack-armed on shore
as those ships slipped to sea,
and stared at each other,
grey-bearded and bent with regret.

But these displaced old war-gods
could still thump their chests
in cane-steadied chorus: "Well,
the gods have bestowed on us
new fighting strengths—
the spear of persuasion, the
power of song, the age-sharpened
eloquence to spin stories
that stir and provoke."

The Old Men of Argos

The moral this tale tells:
Old peacocks still honk. And yet,
those ancient boys were onto something:
arguments do outlive armadas,
songs swords, stories strong-arms.

Madrigals

Larry Beckett

36
told, told
over under my breath as I,
in the union hall,

circling, girls
swimming, in the surf music,
who take it easy,

and I am stung: desire
for paradise, with no, with no

37
language,
till the touch of her tongue,
and the words come

by the old lagoon,
oh our thousand and one kisses
on the airwaves:

last notes, an ocean, over: I must
surface, a sailor; I always hear

38
the siren,
and we conjure, from the long wreck,
our courtship,

that music,
all our sighing, in vain, blowing
in the shrouds

as the years drift, and what remains,
song, radiance of how we fail

Circe: My Story

Diane Averill

Did you really think old Homer, a man,
would get it right when it came to me and Odysseus?
Witch—Enchantress—luring him onto my island?

Odysseus came rushing off his ship of his own free will.
I was simply sunbathing, high on the rocks, when he came to me.
Said I was the most beautiful woman he'd ever met.
Yeah. Sure. Told him I'd met his kind before.
So then he tried some lie about my turning his men into pigs.
Said he had to go after them.

I swear they were already pigs when they landed! I tell you,
the snorting and snuffling, the rooting around my seaweed gardens,
    the odor.
It was almost too much to bear. What would I want with pigs?

Homer did get it right that Hermes popped up and handed Odysseus
tansy, turned them back to men. Idle men with nothing to do. Ghaa!

Odysseus claimed a friend had given him a bag of wind for sailing home,
but had squandered it swimming with mermaids and getting all paranoid about my
friends, the sirens. (They have their story, too.) He didn't really want to return to
"that prude, Penelope," until he'd had some fun.
Stupid windbag with his middle-aged crisis.

Stayed a year, he did, before I called on the Furies to help me out.
Told them all to go to Hell! Homer got that right, only he called it Hades,
in line with the times.

So at last I was alone, and that felt so good I didn't really mind knowing I would go down through the ages in infamy.

Transubstantiation

Precalculus for Christian Schools
    —a book published by Bob Jones University Press (2002).

Cecil Morris

O Christ, they make me shake my head, make me deny more than
    three times
that I know them, these righteous ones, God's auditors, holding His
    words,
His will like blinders before us. They make faith feeble, frail. They clip
so close the Holy Spirit's wings that It must stagger on spindly
bird feet, grounded, something of earth not heaven, something of man.

Take this text as example—a differential math for Christians
who might otherwise miscalculate the precepts of parable.
Must calculus inculcate Christian principles as it teaches
derivatives and integrals? Can we subdivide and sum and
subdivide and sum our way to God, to knowing divine limits?

Grace may be a given, but faith is not a function that resolves
itself through application of Aramaic rules. We will gain
nothing by expressing Ecclesiastes 3:1 as formula.
We can only weaken math and our understanding by turning
this sharp-edged, analytical tool into fuzzy metaphor.

Transubstantiation

Let's not have cookbooks for the Christian palate or financial guides that turn ungodly principal into earthly wealth for Christians or guides for prayer in auto repair. No, don't remind us that faith cannot ignite in us if we are like spark plugs fouled by black sin or that God should set the slope and inclination of our lifeline.

This Just In

Peter Serchuk

I've been reading the sad script of our lives
in the morning paper and don't much care for
the current draft, which churns on and on,
the bloody plot repeating itself over and over,
characters glued to their maniacal insistence
that they live inside of God's head or that
white is king of the rainbow.

We're in desperate need of a rewrite,
heroes we can cheer for and a setting
that's not all smoke and stench. As it stands,
we've got too many villains auditioning for the part;
racing in from bank vaults, pulpits and sand castles,
armed with checkbooks, prayer books and bullets.

Tomorrow, I'm going to skip the main news,
the stock tables and obituaries. I'll skip the jock itch
of the sports page and the costume ball of Hollywood.
Then I'll spread the paper on the floor while I sit
and eat my cereal. And watch my wise and untrained
puppy as he writes his editorial.

What They Did When the Moon Died

Ty Phelps

The bone pile from dinner had just been whisked outside and dumped past the lilac bushes to appease the wolves. They were sitting around the long table, arguing over whose turn it was to make dessert. The chore wheel had been disassembled, again, its pieces hidden around the house. Already Kofi, the meteorologist, and Caroline, the poet, had found pieces in the downstairs toilet tank and tucked inside one of Caroline's underwear balls, respectively. No one could remember who had made dessert beyond the previous Thursday, when Kofi had made apple turnovers and burnt them, and the chore rotation algorithm required at least three weeks of reliable data.

Accusations were hurled. It was nighttime, and Tuesday, and the stars and moon flickered through the wide oval skylight above the dining room.

Then the moon winked out like a squashed candle flame.

Erin, the astrophysicist, saw it happen. She cried out, pointed a trembling finger up to the skylight. The situation was soon confirmed. The moon was gone.

They all jumped up, gawking through the window. Dishes and silverware clattered to the floor. A new chore wheel, half-assembled lazy-susan style on the table, was dashed into pieces. Bernard, the agitator, fell over and bonked his head on the arm of a wooden chair. Erin knelt down to check on him as the rest ran outside, shoving each other in their haste, except Caroline, who refused to budge from her position on the musty sofa by the fireplace in the living room. They circled the house, crying out and gesticulating wildly. A wolf howled and they hurried back indoors.

It had been a crescent moon. The sort of moon one could lounge in like a hammock hung among the constellations.

The constellations, it was noted, were present and accounted for.

Back inside, confusion reigned around the table. They talked over each other, spinning out theories. Bernard went to the kitchen and began sullenly scrubbing pans.

"A new sort of cloud, black, or perhaps even invisible," suggested Kofi, the meteorologist. He sucked lemonade through a straw from a speckled mug.

"Nonsense," said Erin, the astrophysicist. "Fundamental alterations in the nature of gravity." She paced, gnawing on a knuckle. The others kept scooting out of her way.

From the sofa near the fireplace Caroline, the poet, sang out triumphantly, "Another nail in the coffin for God!"

"On the contrary," enjoined Theodore, the priest, fingertips pressed together. High top sneakers poked out from under his black robes and a half-full snifter of brandy sat at his elbow. "Evidence for God's despair."

"I hope the anemones will be alright," said Isabella Maria, the marine biologist, rocking back and forth. She then folded her arms and laughed like a dolphin, which she did whenever she was nervous.

There were six roommates in the house. The seventh, Peter, the astronomer, was away at a conference.

Bernard had been intensely disliked ever since he'd signed all their names, without permission, onto a petition requesting the resignation of a well-respected university president. He knew it, and he'd taken to writing aggressive political slogans on tiny slips of paper and sticking them inside all the dry goods in the pantry. He came in from the kitchen where he had been scrubbing a cake pan crusted with yesterday's dessert. "It's happened," he said, waving the pan at the rest of them. "It's over. The moon is gone. What are we going to do about it?"

This question set off a terrific ruckus. Theodore the priest choked on a sip of brandy trying to reply, and had to be patted on the back by Kofi, who knocked Erin in the ribs with his elbow. Isabella Maria leapt up and ran to the restroom to vomit out of anxiety. From the sofa, Caroline laughed into her milk and composed mental notes about the commotion which she could then cram into her stilted pentameter. Erin slapped Bernard across the cheek, hard. Harder than she usually slapped him. Secret lovers, it was hypothesized. He dropped the pan and it clanged on the floor.

"How can we do anything when we don't understand what's happened?" Erin hissed.

The others nodded seriously.

"There is wisdom there," said Kofi, "but also a kind of apathy."

It was proposed and seconded that additional research was required before any decisions could be reached. Everyone but Bernard vanished into their study nooks and began reading and writing and fiddling with instruments. Bernard rubbed his cheek and returned to the kitchen.

The research stretched into the night. Bernard did the dishes and cleaned the stove. He found the suds and the warm water soothing, savored the feeling of quiet accomplishment that came from moving items from one state of being into another.

Down in the basement, Caroline looked up from her notebook. She'd had three glasses of Theodore's brandy since her dinner milk, and they chased each other around in her stomach in a disconcerting way. She'd scribbled something she was calling "Sonnet of the Insane" while under the influence of what felt like a trance, but may have just been nausea. The verse was lousy, she knew, but she did feel like she had a diamond lurking in one of the anapests. *"And the swells of the oceans replied,"* she kept repeating, sucking on a nubbin of pencil. Topical, she thought, considering the potential implications of the moon's disappearance on the tides.

Up in the attic, Kofi and Erin kept upsetting each other's instruments in their shared workspace. This was a common occurrence, and was accounted for in their margin-of-error analysis by an algorithm that neither of them could sufficiently explain and was thus deemed acceptable. But the agitation of the evening had led to additional disruptions.

Erin was disentangling herself from a low-pressure system simulation mobile (made of pipe-cleaners and poster board cutouts of thunder clouds, which she had built for a presentation at a local elementary school) when Kofi drew his head back from their powerful shared telescope.

"No particle disbursement," he said.

"Not an explosion then," Erin said, nodding. She went downstairs to cross the scenario off the master list, which Isabella Maria had set up in the kitchen.

The list, written in orange and blue marker on a huge pad of paper, sat on an easel near the dining room table, just to the right of

Isabella Maria's study nook, which itself was fenced on two sides by bookshelves and on the third by her eight-foot long aquarium. Erin struck through "Exploded." Also crossed out were "made invisible by human science" and "end of an elaborate hoax that there was ever a moon in the first place." Historical and scientific evidence for the dismissal of each scenario was cited at the bottom of the paper.

Someone had also struck through "Act of God," which had then been rewritten below, and then struck through again, and then rewritten again. Isabella Maria claimed no knowledge of it and suggested that it likely happened when she was tending her aquarium, a task which always occupied her full attention, or perhaps during her frequent trips to the bathroom.

Meanwhile, Theodore was in his priest's hole where he kept his secret apocrypha, through which everyone else had rummaged at one time or another. He was reading the Qur'an, and also St. Thomas Aquinas, and also Charles Muggeridge, though he considered the latter a vapid twat who made miracles out of molehills. He lit incense and fondled his prayer beads and thought about whether self-flagellation would be appropriate. Perhaps if they didn't have answers by the weekend.

After finishing the dishes, Bernard went out in his pickup truck and distributed leaflets about the dangers of neoliberalism around a well-to-do neighborhood in the town twenty miles south of their house. He did this several times a week, especially when he sensed possible upheaval. A literally cosmic event surely qualified, he felt, and he expected a better reception than usual.

By midnight, Kofi had given up on his investigation of weather patterns and was tending to the internet on the big computer console in the living room, kitty-corner to Isabella Maria's study nook. The keyboard was a bit sticky because Caroline had dripped jam on it two days prior. Articles seethed across the screen. The tides had stopped at a low point, causing a wave of concern from biologists and fishing industry experts. The pagans were in despair and were converting to assorted monotheisms at a record rate. Photographs of the last eclipse were selling for six-figure sums at auction. New non-lunar calendar systems were being proposed and rejected. The nihilists were gleefully rewriting nursery rhymes: *hey diddle diddle the cat and the fiddle the cow jumped over nothing.* A publisher solicited moon-themed submissions for an emergency poetry anthology. The environmentalists and their adversaries were blasting pithy visual attacks at each other in the most alarming way. Petitions were circulating. One howled to save now-exposed coral reefs by any means necessary, including saltwater bucket brigades. Another was titled "Fuck the reefs, cement shall be our salvation!" A third, in bold font and tepid prose, advised compromise.

Kofi reluctantly called over Bernard, who upon return from his leaflet distribution had been prowling impatiently around the master list, to show him another internet proposal. It pushed for the immediate construction of a moon replacement to be hoisted and set into the putative gravity gap that now existed in space's fabric by a process known as the "God-Lever." This was the brain-child of a once-respected engineer and theologian who'd been disgraced by his innumerable sex scandals with a series of undergraduates.

"They've got to bring religion into everything," Bernard growled in disgust.

Erin came over. "The religion's irrelevant. It won't work. The lever itself has to be of such size that the force necessary to move it on its fulcrum requires a weight heavier than the moon itself."

What They Did When the Moon Died

Kofi nodded, wondering privately how the lack of tides would affect weather patterns.

"Will the dearth of ocean stimulation result in less evaporation and thus fewer rain clouds?" he wondered aloud. Erin and Bernard nodded in unison, convinced. Drought was likely, they decided. Increased economic instability. Famine. Insanity. Disruption of the social order. Bernard ran off to print new pamphlets about how periods of crisis are the best time to create direct-action, mutual-aid alternatives to cumbersome government structures. Erin yelled at his retreating back that he was wasting his time. Kofi began ordering non-perishable food online.

The master list of moon-disappearance theories had grown thick in the middle of the paper as the proposed causes grew more grandiose, and then tapered into exhausted, inchoate fragments:

Glitter

Time-delayed erosion

Elevator doors

Hell On Earth

Space Quake

Fairies

Teeth

Back in the living room, Caroline was composing a sestina, badly, pacing and writing on the periwinkle walls with a whiteout pen. She slugged from a flask she had filled with Theodore's brandy. She hadn't composed anything except for listing the end words, which she was writing in huge letters all around the walls: *Gut rot, Quest, Lunar, Idiom, Troll, Celibate*. Their order eluded her, which made her feel like James Joyce for a pleasurable minute.

The faucet dripped. Bernard had forgotten to fix it, again. Isabella Maria was inconsolable, running from her aquarium to the bathroom and back again. Someone had emailed her a series of pictures of dying starfish, stuck in now permanently uncovered tide pools, the sight of which had aggravated her irritable bowel syndrome. She wanted desperately to cuddle her own sea creatures to her breast, tell them it would be alright, that they would do something, that the humans could handle it, but she couldn't take them out of the aquarium without killing them. She should've bought that salamander she'd seen at the pet store last summer. She could have cuddled it for at least a little while. Instead she dipped two fingers into the water and waited for the fish to notice her. She hadn't been this upset since Caroline had shaved her head while she was sleeping and used her dark curls to make a wig for a taxidermied manta ray which was then displayed prominently on the mantle. Kofi eventually decided the whole thing was too vicious and had had the ray and wig incinerated.

They all slept rottenly that night, except Caroline, who passed out gleefully on the living room floor. Isabella Maria was woken up at 5:00 when someone threw a cucumber through her window, shattering the glass and filling the room with a refreshing smell.

In the morning, it was discovered that the president had called a meeting of her cabinet. There was to be a press conference that night, according to the articles that Kofi had left up on the computer. He was busy making breakfast, trying to cheer up Isabella Maria, beside herself with anxiety about the cucumber incident, with huevos rancheros. The clatter in the kitchen and the smell of coffee gradually drew the rest of them towards the living room, except Theodore, who stayed locked in his priest's hole. He had fallen asleep with his rosary in his mouth; and Caroline, who continued to snore. The others stepped over her.

"What's wrong?" asked Erin quietly to Bernard when they met in the kitchen. They had spent a surreptitious hour of adequate lovemaking in Erin's room in the moments before dawn. Bernard had then climbed down the gutter and crawled through the first floor bathroom window before sneaking off to his own bed.

"Someone threw a cucumber through Isabella Maria's bedroom window early this morning," Bernard said, and poured coffees all around. The others offered grudging thanks. Kofi was burning the eggs and swearing.

"What's that supposed to be? A threat?" Erin stirred in powdered creamer.

"Something to do with the reefs, I guess. That's what Isabella Maria thinks."

Erin frowned. "What does a cucumber have to do with the reefs?"

"What does anything have to do with anything?" mumbled Caroline, who had woken up and now lay face down on the carpet.

After breakfast, the research resumed. The cucumber/window incident was added to the scope of their inquiries. Caroline finally stood up at 10:00 and began revising the six words of her white-out poem. The master list hadn't any new entries, other than two more salvos from the "Act of God" combatants. The original supposition, that the back and forth was due to Theodore and Caroline, was thrown out when they realized that Theodore hadn't been seen by anyone in hours, and that Caroline had been passed out drunk. Bernard was now assumed to have played both roles in the contest to drum up conflict.

Despondency was mounting. Caroline offered to read some sonnets she'd written about the liberation inherent in a life lived without certainties. Bernard offered to facilitate a workshop on how to best attack police in riot gear. Kofi and Erin offered tips about maintaining the ability to theorize in the face of despair. Isabella Maria offered to check on Theodore in his hole, and he emerged thoroughly rumpled, his rosary still firmly lodged in his mouth. Though he refused to speak, he pantomimed his willingness to lead a silent prayer session and handed them a sermon written in purple crayon about the dangers of masturbation.

At 4:00 p.m., Peter the astronomer called and announced that he had run off with a painter from Bulgaria. He wouldn't be coming back, but he would mail his portion of the rent. It was an exciting time to be an astronomer, he could say with confidence. This event was bound to breathe new life into the field. He planned on using the moon's disappearance as the centerpiece of his forthcoming space opera. He asked how everyone was doing, and apologized for the prank with the chore wheel. Isabella Maria hung up on him.

When the president made her announcement that night, they all gathered around the computer. Bernard was forced to stand in the back for his putative role in the master list Act-of-God-debacle. Kofi turned on the speakers and clicked on the live stream.

The president's podium was covered in flags. A microphone poked out from its top like a stubborn cowlick. Behind the podium, a vast collage of astronauts and robots on star-spangled backing was hung, bunched at the corners and gently sagging in the middle. Three large men in suits and sunglasses loomed at the periphery, touching ear-pieces and scowling.

The president appeared to wild, fearful applause. She stooped her tall, thin frame over the microphones and cleared her throat. There was an expectant hush from the crowd. Bernard coughed and the others glared at him.

"In times of great change," the President began, her almost-Adam's-apple bobbing as she spoke, "when the very foundations of our reality seem suddenly unreliable, when the nature of the universe is suddenly in question, in times such as these, it is imperative that we step boldly into the unknown and take action." She paused for emphasis. Her arms fluttered, stork-like, to the sides and her hands lifted towards the empty sky.

"After all," she continued, "it was action that won the Revolution, that conquered the Midwestern prairies and distant mountains, that sent us into the ultimate mystery of space."

Bernard harrumphed in disgust. "Typical exceptionalism narrative. What a crock." The others shushed him.

"And so we're going to build the God-Lever," said the president. "We are currently constructing a pair of rockets that will carry the necessary construction materials for the lever, and we are repositioning several space stations to serve as the fulcrums upon which the lever can operate. Our finest chemists are at work creating artificial moon rock, which will be shipped in segments up to the space station for assembly." The crowd cheered. "Not only will we repair this new hole in our beloved cosmos, we will improve on nature's design. And this great project will stand as a triumph on human ingenuity that all the world can gaze upon in wonder and pride." The crowd cheered again, and string quartet music began slowly swelling in the background. "The world is watching. Seventeen nations have signed on to assist in this project. More will undoubtedly follow. And," said the President, pausing for emphasis, "this project will create thousands of new jobs." Thunderous applause greeted this announcement.

Kofi turned off the computer and the scene disappeared. They all looked at each other, except Caroline, who was writing couplets on her shoes with a blue marker.

"Idiocy," said Erin.

No one spoke. Kofi and Erin made half-hearted calculations on some nearby napkins, attempting to discredit the God-Lever. After finishing her shoes, Caroline rolled herself like a log into the kitchen. Kofi balled his napkin up and threw it at the computer. He got up to leave, but Erin grabbed his arm.

"Wait!" she said. "Given this new information, and the scope of our individual research, and the perspective afforded by a full day inhabiting this new equilibrium, we ought to hold a synthesis meeting. Caroline, take notes. Bernard, make coffee." The others sprang up. Caroline began practicing how to jot corporate shorthand in dactylic hexameter. Theodore began speaking all the words he'd saved up, in alphabetical order. Kofi gathered up papers and instruments. Bernard burned his thumb on the tea kettle.

Isabella Maria sat by the computer, quietly sobbing. Her beloved sea creatures, marooned and afraid in the now-stilled oceans.

"What are we going to *do?*" she cried, but the meeting had started and the others didn't hear.

Outside past the lilac bushes, the wolves howled. Though at what no one could accurately say.

Death Keeps a Garden

Chelsea Thiel

Planted in up-turned eyes, stargazers peer through a lens. The yolk of cracked moon, spying on a skeleton's tango round the tiger lapping sundew from the pitcher plants grown wild feeding on the fly's fingertips. The bouquet resting in the toad's throat plays like a trumpet blast announcing the arrival of the sultan who bows and nods his cranial cap to the purple Turks. From the lemon bursts the snake's head—white—and curled round the base the Alpine tree that has turned to swamp wood. At the center—embedded in the intimate tissue of the host cell—the corpse lily flourishes.

The Real Truth about Winter

Marie Hartung

No one talks about the brutality of January,
how she walks like a carcass, littering crows
and burn on the sunset. How she canopies
the sky with wounds, emptying it of light.

Nobody comprehends the shame of snow
falling on the ocean, filling inflamed gills
with endless lead, scalding its salt-tears
into nonsensical poetry no one can rehearse.

In my backyard, the sun's last sentence
tranquilizes evening with syntax errors,
pours grief into heaps of paralyzed leaves,
and down pinhole barrels of hardened stalks.

No one categorizes the sparkle of morning.
The falseness of a low horizon promises
something better—anything better—even though
winter blanches our sinew, bitter and bloody stars.

The Real Truth about Winter

In the end, daylight is not what we asked for.
Only unknown words cast as gravity, to tether
us to the concrete darkness filling our lungs,
until we finally learn the truth about drowning.

Dirtwork: The Spring Campaign

Tim Gillespie

I scrape from the raised bed the winter-rot,
my escape from the canker of politics inside,
then rake in manure, mulch-ready the garden box,
a break from the rancor and shit of the news.

I divide the dug-up dahlia bulbs of last fall,
fortify the dark soil, replant the bulbs in the reek,
pulverize any dirt clods, tamp down my ire,
and side with the tubers biding their time.

Later I tug off in the basement my mud-boots,
trudge upstairs, take root at my desk,
slug out letters to editors, sign petitions,
join the scrum and the spew of that world.

I'm aggrieved by this truth: as my soil now
needs amending, so does the world's hard ground.
The tea kettle boils and howls to be heeded.
The garden needs tending. I'm breeding just outrage.

Dirtwork: The Spring Campaign

My nudgings of nature in my little earth-patch
leave gunk under my nails, dirt-smutch and blood.
The crud and the blight on TV seeps deeper—
hard to scrub, toxic, ceaseless, dumb.

I know rage can overgrow joy in the garden,
take hold—relentless weed—if it's nurtured and fed,
but oh, when I'm readying my last box of dirt,
let me be sowing dahlias instead.

A Horse in Custer's Column Survives at Little Bighorn

Matthew J. Spireng

He served well and without complaint
ridden hard day after day in pursuit
of the Indian. The grass was sometimes dry

and brittle, the water, though sweet and clear,
distant between its holds. That day he smelled
the ponies, and others did as well—evident

in every snort and whinny. But still they served,
following the lead of their riders, quickening their pace
though they were worn, some lame, all knowing

there were more ahead than they'd ever found before.
It was on that ridge, Indians and ponies all around,
the crack of rifles and shouts and screams of men, his rider

down to steady his aim, that he reared and galloped off.
Call it fear or call it horse sense, but when Custer
ordered his men to shoot the horses

A Horse in Custer's Column Survives at Little Bighorn

and stack their bodies to form a wall,
it was clear that what that horse had done was
best to do. Even as an Indian took his reins

and steadied him, he heard the guns and turned
to see the soldiers' horses drop as if
lightning had struck them all at once. Standing

one moment proudly with men, then shot down
by their riders. After, he was led off
to share brief peace with the ponies,

the only horse of those on the ridge not killed
in battle or shot by the man it carried there, not
of its own accord, but because the man commanded.

Austerity

Simon Anton Niño Baena

The summer before the war,
when the tourists returned
one last time, I knelt down
and prayed at the city's grotto,
lighted candles on its altar.
With the rest of the penitents
I emptied the wine casks
in the outlying villages.
I poured pig's blood
on the cauldron after mass
and let the fiesta commence
where I fell the trees
and bequeathed
a denuded landscape
to our estranged children.
I honored the dead
by ignoring their lessons.
Now the shadow
of spires at dusk
mirrors the sunset
in our eyes.

Austerity

Around the corner
outside a rundown cafe,
I line up and beg,
like a dog,
for a few coins.

For crumbs.

The Picnic

Francis Opila

Six old Polish women wear babushkas,
walk slowly past fallow fields,
carry woven baskets,
bouquets of tulips, yellow and scarlet.
The path opens onto a sedge meadow,
blackbirds peck at dandelions,
ants crawl religiously over stones.
It's Sunday—there are no chores,
the duty of Mass is already done.
They find their place in the afternoon sun,
unfurl plaid wool blankets,
lay out flowers and food,
settle aching bones on hard ground
with no complaint.
They say grace, callused hands
folded at their waists,
they partake of bread, sausage,
bits of cheese. Talk comes in spurts,
between grass-blown silence,
thoughts about their fallen men,
about whom they dare not speak.

The Picnic

The matriarch opens a bottle of red wine,
six cups raise to toast, but don't touch.
The youngest starts to hum, but stops—
gusts of wind rise,
quivering day turns to dusk,
they gather their belongings,
fold the plaid blankets.
Tulip petals, yellow and scarlet,
fall to the ground.

Waiting Stops

Will Radke

M̲y upstairs neighbor Rebecca comes over late. Most days she slides a handwritten note under my front door.

I save every note. I'll never tell her that. I don't want it to affect what she says. Nobody writes notes. I know this is ours. What I'll never have, or want, with anyone else.

"Are you sure you can't, Carter?" Rebecca asks again.

We're standing on our shared front porch. We live in an old two-flat in Lincoln Park. I'm having a smoke and Rebecca's trying to get me to go to someplace called Lincoln Station with her and her friends.

I can't remember how to handle all that. I say I have work to finish, which is what I usually tell her. That or I'm tired. I ran out of excuses before I made the first one up.

The sun's close and everywhere. It's right in my eyes. I tap my shirt pocket. My sunglasses aren't there. I squint. I shield my eyes and look at Rebecca.

She's wearing a blue sundress with orange flowers all over it. Knee-high brown boots. Her purse matches her boots and her dark hair is down and wavy.

"Can't you finish in the morning?" asks Rebecca.

I shake my head no and light another smoke.

Rebecca still doesn't believe that working from home doing paperwork for my grandpa's construction company is a real job. She's going to be a senior at DePaul this fall. Next year she plans on going to graduate school. I can understand why she doesn't think I have a real job.

"I really wanna introduce you to all my friends, baby. You should at least meet up with us later."

"This is gonna take awhile," I admit.

"Try to come later," she says. "We'll be out late. It'll be fun, I promise."

I wouldn't know what to do. What to talk to about, how fully to answer questions. I don't know what goes on anymore—never did, really. So, eventually, I just stopped. Maybe I never started.

I use one of my apartment's two bedrooms, the bigger one, as an office. There are two bookshelves against one wall, filled with novels and short story collections. A few were written by my older brother Jones. The rest Jones gave to me. The books aren't gifts. They're homework assignments. Once he reads them he drops them off at my place for me to read so he has someone to discuss them with.

My desk is across the room from the bookshelves. On it is a draft of Jones's most recent short story. Fourteen pages, written in his chicken-scratch handwriting with a pencil, held together by a paperclip.

Editing my brother's fiction is my second job. He thinks I should edit his stories first and breathe some other time. It's more time-consuming than my job. But after Jones reads what I write about his stories, he pays me with insults and temper tantrums. It's worth it. Gramps only gives me money.

The story I'm working on now is about us, when Jones was ten and I was eight, before he wrote fiction but after he knew he was a writer, when we lived our summers riding bikes, going to the library, watching and playing baseball.

    I'm trying to get back into it. I want to. I always want to go back. But every time I start to read, everything shifts to Rebecca. Those dresses she wears. The way she tastes, feels, loves. I can't talk about it. My head's going to fly off. All my patience is gone. Until she comes back later, I'm going to be worthless.

I go for a walk to clear my head. It's the first evening the day's heat hasn't gone away and so the neighborhood's busier than usual. People heading home from work, others going out for dinner or drinks. All the outdoor tables are filled up. Friends together laughing and drinking. Cold beer, bottles perspiring. Colorful summer drinks in tall glasses. I guess it's warm enough to drink those, but I don't know. Reminds me of kids so anxious for summer that they wear shorts to school on the first spring day the temperature rises above fifty. Reminds me that even though our toys change the way we play does not. Reminds me of riding bikes with Jones for what felt like days at a time. Riding until we were struggling to catch our breaths and our muscles felt like putty.

    Back home, on the front porch, I sit in my old folding lawn chair with the green and white vinyl webbing and listen to the Cubs game on my portable radio.

    It's such a perfect night to sit outside. A subtle breeze, a cloudless sky. The moon, low, big, and bright. The first hot night this June. The Cubs game goes on and the darkness settles in and I read Rebecca's three sentence note again and again and look up every time I hear someone walking down the block. Time has always moved slowly for me but waiting for her, it almost stops.

Rebecca comes back from the bathroom. Naked except for her boots. Those boots. She looks unbelievable in those boots. Her long legs. That dark hair. There's so much of it. It goes halfway down her back. I want it everywhere. Sitting on the edge of the bed, I stare like I could never look at anyone else.

"What're you doing tomorrow?" she asks as she walks over.

"Working."

She sits on my lap and kisses me.

"I meant after."

"I don't know."

"I was thinking that maybe tomorrow night we could maybe go out for dinner," she says, her words blending together.

"Out for dinner?"

"Yeah, you know, it's this new thing that people do together. Groups of friends, couples. They go to a place called a restaurant. A host takes them to a table and then a waiter takes their drink and food orders. A bartender makes their drinks and chefs cook their food, and the waiter brings it all to them so they can relax and talk, enjoy each other's company without worrying about cooking or cleaning or anything. Everyone's doing it, Carter. It's a blast."

I want to smile.

"What's wrong?"

I shrug.

"Fine," she says, and gets up. "Let's go out Friday or Saturday night."

She's standing in front of me. I'm looking up. Her beauty absolutely wrecks me.

"You can talk to me," she says.

I feel so, too, but I don't talk. I stare across at the beige wall with no picture hanging from it. My entire place is empty like this. I could leave right now with nothing and nobody would know it was me living in this apartment.

"Is it me?" she asks. "You seem fine spending time with me here."

I nod.

"And you have a good time, don't you?"

I nod again.

"But you won't go out with me?"

"I didn't say that," I say.

"You haven't said much."

"I know."

"Are you embarrassed of me?"

"Why would I be embarrassed of you?"

"Because I'm like ten years younger than you."

"I'm not embarrassed of you."

"Did you go out for dinner with Hannah?"

This is the last thing I want to hear. Not only now, but ever. Rebecca believes it's necessary to know everything about each other. I don't. Some things just need to be over. So I haven't told Rebecca anything more than a basic outline: that Hannah and I were together for a number of years and had a house plant and a mortgage and every kind of debt—that our ending was fucked and she hasn't seen me since I walked out that night.

But now I wish I'd never mentioned Hannah at all. You can't start over when your past is always being pulled into the present.

"You don't want to be exclusive," Rebecca claims, and slips her dress back on.

"I'm not seeing anyone else. Are you?"

"Don't turn this around."

"What?"

"You just accused me of dating other people when that's not the issue," she explains.

"What's the issue?"

"That *you* don't want to be with me, Carter—you just want to sleep with me."

"That's not true."

"Then let's go out for dinner tomorrow. Let's go out for drinks right now."

"I've told you, I don't do that."

"You're the most frustrating person in the world, do you know that? The most frustrating. I'm sure that's why she left you too," she says and walks out of my bedroom.

I get up and go after her.

"Rebecca," I say.

She stops in the hallway, turns around. "What?"

"Don't go."

"Why?"

"I don't want you to," I say. "Spend the night," I tell her. "I want to wake up next to you."

"You make me feel so cheap," she tells me, turns around and walks out.

I'm reading in bed. I guess I'm not reading. I'm holding a book, but I'm not reading it. I can't even look at the page. I'm finally in Jones's story. That day with my brother when those two older kids stole our bikes, and as they were riding away, Jones, pissed as hell yet poised as always, picked up a golf-ball-sized rock and threw it at them, hitting one in the back, making him scream but not stopping him from riding away, and how later when Jones told the story to our friends the rock hit the kid in the back of the head and knocked him off the bike and we watched him kneeling on the pavement, tossing out every swear there is, doing that through tears as blood, lots of blood—Jones always emphasized how much blood there was—poured down his neck and all over his white undershirt, and that because we didn't want to get in trouble we ran away, without our bikes, but that, Jones said, didn't matter for shit.

Rebecca's bedroom is right above mine. I can't believe I started something with a neighbor. I knew if things didn't work out we'd still see each other. Any night she could come home or leave when I'm sitting on the front porch. Ruin that place for me. That eventually, and probably soon, I'd see her with another man.

I knew all these things before I kissed her for the first time. But the future didn't matter in that moment. I was only thinking about one thing. Rebecca's the same age Hannah was when I fell in love with her. I thought that might be it. An age when love comes on the strongest, comes on so fully you can never get it all out of you. I thought that even though I'm not the right age with a girl who is I could get it back and stop living with having had it stolen from me.

More than ever, I know I should've followed my brother's lead. I should've picked up something. Something hard like a rock. Whatever was there to be picked up and thrown. Used to smash in his face. You've already lost, you still fight. There's always something to fight for. I shouldn't have just walked away with that guy lying next to Hannah in our bed. I should've made his heart bleed into his gut like mine was.

I go outside for a smoke, shut the front door hard enough to hear without slamming it.

Cooler now, the wind, blowing in from the lake, has picked up, making tree branches whip back and forth and putting out my lighter's flame as I try to light a cigarette.

I finally get one going. I stand on the top step of the porch and smoke and look out at the street lined with cars parked bumper to bumper that won't move until morning. I take out the note. I read it and refold it and put it back in my pocket. In my head, I hear Rebecca say, "you make me feel so cheap," for the hundredth time since she left. It's Nora all over again.

"This isn't going anywhere, Carter. You're unavailable," Nora said.

Me, I thought it was because Nora was ten years older.

And Alice, she lived too far away. Jessica drank too much. Beth chain-smoked and never slept. Cecilia only talked about her dreams, and would always ask, what do you think that means, like they could ever mean anything to me.

I can't hold off until morning.

I head upstairs and stand in front of Rebecca's door. But I don't knock. I stare at the door, thinking, not feeling the way I think I should feel, feeling like I'm not in the right place, when suddenly, all this waiting stops.

It Could Have Turned Out Different in a Different Story

Marie Hartung

When the personal attorney started talking
after the sentencing and the moment
where all was lost anyway—the money,
the job, the girls—we discussed loyalty.

But it wasn't exactly that. You sat like Saturday morning
on an Adirondack next to me at the brewery campfire
or also years earlier, naked in the soaking pool,
and confessed a warning: the sky I had my knuckles

scraping was really inky torn skin, a blackish
pooling around a wound on the inside.
And you told me it would always be this way.
I knew, without admission, you were spooling truth.

Just as we were beginning to sleep together
in the silence and chaos of the sweat-soaked fire,
you continuously blew toward that flesh I tried
too hard to hold. I heard words past the wreckage owned

It Could Have Turned Out Different in a Different Story

and I surreptitiously borrowed. In both cases,
the moon lit the charred sky. So much promise
now calligraphy on the blade of autumn's flesh cruelly
rusting winters' final edge. But your breathing

should have been the clue. Your exhale, my inhale—
syncopated. It wasn't the raw, aching flesh
I was after. But the light I tasted on my tongue,
sweet and sour candy I wanted so badly to unfold me.

And like the attorney, I knew I would take a bullet
for you in every flesh-eating, scorched sky dream
I clutched. What blinds us, I learned,
is the body climaxing inside a redrafted story

the tabloid tell-all where night and day
become indistinguishable from regret—
a host nibbling between our bodies,
a cascade of rain separating our wind-soaked lips.

Poetry and Sex

Mark Rubin

Repetition is good for the soul, so here we are
again, in Montreal's Montecristo Cigar Bar.
Where there is smoke

there is a blond waitress on fire,
men dreaming of mouth-to-mouth
resuscitation. My dad is there too,

a Chihuahua dreaming of Great Danehood,
a gray whiskered dog barking
at passing cars. He is teaching me the ropes

or the knots they make. I'm not sure
if he hates to be alone or fears
he is, like cargo waiting on a train

stalled at a foggy, main-line railway stop,
the station master clicking his pen,
10 across: *a r s p o e t i c a.*

Poetry and Sex

In Quebec in the Montecristo Cigar Bar
there is low-end booze and behold,
here she comes, Umbriana, a bliss

of tremulous light with pouty lips.
Their cards are played
before they're dealt. My dad winks,

Two Bombay martinis. Her tongue peeks out
slow as original sin, a primal cue
poetry and sex are conceptual yearnings.

To which he adds, *in-out with a twist.*

Unruly

Taylor Gaede

glossy arachnid
on the half-moon window
creating a long shadow
larger than Father's hands.

silkworm nest
eating holes in leaves
and fraying silk strings
to catch spindly fingers.

sharp-suited yellowjacket
drowsily floating
on murky wings
stinging calloused palms.

swallowtail butterfly
caught between little hands
fluttering softly
leaving powder-dust scales.

Beirut

David Mihalyov

Matt traced the long scratch on the hood of Craig's car with his index finger, imagining what could have etched the serpentine mark. A coin perhaps, or, more exotically, a knife. Whatever it was, it had done its job as the paint sported a scar that no amount of buffing would heal. He shifted his attention from the car to the beer he was holding, taking a drink and wiping his mouth with the back of a hand.

"Did you hear about Ron Dixon?" he asked.

"Nope."

The two were perched on the hood of the car, a six pack of Genny Light between them. The metal was still warm and the engine ticked while cooling. They had parked in a small lot beside their old elementary school, which made their actions feel somewhat wrong to them, even though it was nearly midnight.

"He was killed in that bombing in Beirut."

"No shit." Craig looked up. "I guess I knew he had joined the Marines but I didn't know he was over there." He paused and took a sip. "That sucks."

"I don't think I could find Beirut on a map."

Despite the seriousness of what he had just heard, Craig snorted a laugh. "Idiot," he said. "It's in the Middle East."

"But what the hell are our Marines doing there? We're not in any war."

"Dunno."

Craig assumed it had something to do with Israel and the PLO, maybe terrorism, but he couldn't remember any hijackings lately. And reading the newspaper had slowed since he started his current job.

"Do you remember playing little league ball on the field back there?" Matt asked, waving his half empty can in the general direction he referred to.

"Yeah, I just remember it always had mosquitos. Didn't Ron play baseball back then?"

"He did. He was pretty good, too. Then he got more interested in partying and getting drunk."

"I don't think I said more than two words to him all through senior year."

"We used to trade baseball cards back in junior high." Matt smiled at a memory. "He was a huge Dodgers fan for some reason, and I used to get pretty much whatever I wanted for a Steve Garvey or Davey Lopes."

"He was always a prick to me."

"He was a prick to pretty much everyone. I guess I got along with him OK."

"Like attracts like."

Craig finished his beer and threw his empty like he would a football, the can arcing through the air before bouncing a few times on the blacktop, the tinny sound making a nearby dog bark, the noises louder at this hour. The silver in the can reflected light from the moon, which made Craig lean back against the windshield and look up. Although it was relatively warm for a late October night he was chilled, wondering if he should have another beer, knowing he had to get up way too early for work. The decision was made for him as he

Beirut

heard the pop and pull as Matt opened another can. Always better when someone else makes the call. Without looking he reached his arm out until he felt the still cold metal against his palm. He thought about Ron Dixon and the first memory that came to mind was ninth grade, carrying his folders and books under his arm between classes, and having Ron come up from behind and knock them out. Even now Craig's cheeks flushed at the image of him bent down, trying to grab the scattered mess as dozens of legs moved around him, most trying to avoid, a few making his job more difficult, all, he felt, judging him and his lack of character for letting this happen without fighting back.

"Hard to believe someone our age is dead," Matt said.

Craig took a long sip before answering. "Yeah," was all he could say.

"How do you go from here to dead? I can't even comprehend that." Matt turned to look at Craig, more serious than he had been all night. "I mean, I get it. One of my grandfathers died a couple of years ago, but he was old."

"I've had a couple of aunts and uncles die, but they lived out of state and I never really knew them."

"But Ron, man. I think they were all asleep when that truck smashed through the gates. Maybe the noise woke them up but then all of a sudden there was an explosion and they were dead."

"Maybe it's better that way." Craig paused to consider what he had just said.

"Maybe, I don't know. Jerry still won't talk about what happened in Vietnam."

Jerry was Matt's oldest brother, older by a decade, which at one point made Matt think he was a mistake of sorts, his parents too old to actively want another child, especially a fourth. A loser in the draft lottery, Jerry had spent a year in the army.

"He always scared me when I was younger," Craig said. "Something about his eyes freaked me out."

"Me too. I was ten years old or so when he got back and I remember him having nightmares all the time, screaming a lot."

"Must have been crazy."

Craig's knowledge of the war came mostly from movies and a general interest in the '60s, a time he often felt he missed out on, a feeling that he was born too late. He loved the music, the pictures of hippie women with long flowing hair and smiles from being high. He understood that his views were more romantic than realistic but that didn't change his interest. Or the niggling thought that he was not living through a memorable time. He didn't move here from the old country not speaking any English, he didn't scuffle through the Depression, or fight in World War II, Korea, or Vietnam. Sure, the Cold War was still going but the fear of nuclear attack was almost non-existent and he couldn't even laugh at memories of school drills to prepare for a bomb.

"You know what's crazy?" Matt asked?

"What?" Craig was jerked back into October 1983.

"I'm pretty much the same age Jerry was when he went over. I can't imagine being in a war, being shot at every day, going on patrol every night, walking through rice paddies and jungles not knowing if every step would be my last." He paused for a moment, staring down. "I used to wonder what it was like in a war, how I would react. In some way I guess I wanted to believe I would be a hero."

Craig sat up as best he could and looked at his friend, someone he had known for most of his life.

"Bud," he said. "this is the most serious I think I've ever seen you."

"Well, shit, it's death. Ron Dixon does not exist anymore. He will never get married, never have kids. You'll never get to know him as an adult and realize maybe he wasn't a prick. It's all so fucking random."

The randomness of life was something Craig had been pondering for a while now. Here he was, sitting on the hood of his car with his best friend on a late October evening drinking beer while Ron Dixon was dead. Not that he had had any desire of joining the Marines, but Craig believed he was doing nothing to rationalize why he existed. He knew the world wasn't a great place, although he lived with the vague notion that it was better for him than for most. And he knew those memorable times he hadn't lived through were mostly hard. The reason he spent much of his waking life working in a kitchen was that he couldn't handle college, not that he didn't have the opportunity or couldn't afford it or have a way to get there or had parents who thought school was a waste of time and money. It was all on him. He noticed that Matt had slid off the car and was walking toward the playground.

"Hey, where are you going? he called. "I need to be at work at six,"

Matt didn't respond, he kept going until he reached the swings and then sat down. For a moment he only moved his legs, rocking in place, and then he gave a stronger push and started to actually swing. The chains screeched in protest, Matt's weight more than they were accustomed to. The neighborhood dog began to bark again while Craig watched his friend swoop higher, legs pumping almost in anger. Matt continued to awkwardly hold his beer as the arc increased, hypnotically, and the entire structure shuddered with each pass. He reached the point where, from Craig's vantage point, his body cleared the moon, which was a few days past full. Craig closed his eyes and listened to the back and forth rhythmic squeal. He knew his friend well enough to let him be, that what was bothering him needed to come out as much as possible in physical activity. He smiled at the memory of Matt racing around the neighborhood on his bike when something traumatic happened, such as losing a driveway basketball game. Then he sat up with the premonition that Matt would soon let go and fly through the night sky, completing a parabola started with the upward motion of the swing. Instead, Matt screamed for a few seconds and then started scraping his feet on the ground to slow his momentum, eventually coming to a stop. Craig watched him sit there with his chest heaving, too far away to ascertain if it was from exertion or crying, wondering if he should walk over and attempt to offer comfort or if he should stay on the car and give his friend some sense of privacy. Matt looked defeated.

They both knew it was time to leave. Craig got into the driver's seat as Matt slowly walked toward him, picking up Craig's empty can and throwing it in the backseat when reaching the car.

"You OK?"

"Yeah," Matt answered.

Craig thought he still looked emotional but didn't know what to say. Matt played with the car radio until he found a song he could handle. He then sat back in his seat and closed his eyes. Craig left the parking lot, picturing one last time the two of them, ten or twelve years ago, running around on the playground.

"We used to love this place," he said.

"I still do."

"I assume you're done for the night?" He was driving in the general direction of home.

"No. And neither are you."

Craig raised his eyebrows in surprise.

"You are going to figure out the meaning of life and, once you do, you are going to explain it to me. But since I intend to get drunk I likely won't remember, so you probably should write it down so I can read it later."

"Huh," Craig said. "I guess I have my work cut out for me."

"You surely do," Matt said. He turned up the radio and opened another can. "We both do."

My Best Friend's Secret

Christine DeSimone

On our New Orleans vacation, she vomited oysters:
their plucked and buttered flesh gleamed on pavement.

I sit her up, rearrange her loose bones.
All of her mornings wear forced perfume; tall empties

stand fierce on black countertops.
The veins in her eyes say, *I just need to get to Friday.*

Her lies require a certain economy:
they wear her mascara to breakfast.

I boil her in oil. I cut her out.
She holds my dumb tongue in her hands.

She is the corner of my loneliness.
She is my own silent song.

She is barely held together
by silk and ocean air.

My Best Friend's Secret

We live on the same street
but walk home in different directions.

If her hopes stay high enough,
she thinks she will never die:

She closes her eyes to keep from falling.
She clutches the edge of her grassy earth.

My Her/Him Hirman

Mark Rubin

To have mind-body connected by a flange,
a swelling in the skin, a delicacy to an ant,

to be deaf, blind, and burdened
by five hearts

to be gender fluidly packed
into one accordion tube

to rub shamelessly in the dark, sticky
in old-fashioned ways, nibbled

from either end
as one might a strand of pasta

to be pulled from one's home, impaled
by bird beak, hook, or needle-poked on paraffin

is to be on earth for the taking
of earth.

My Her/Him Hirman

I hear my mother's finger's voice,
B-sharp ascending, *Who ate the Velveeta?*

as if the worm I kept as a pet preferred it
over dirt, dung, and leaf rot.

You Are Not Who You Are

Taylor Gaede

Snakeskin in the toolshed
shredded at the edges
clinging to flat tires
and cobwebs.
the farmer takes a pitchfork
to toss it over the fence.

that same snake
slinks back
skin black obsidian
eyes midnight tide.
it encircles the backyard tree
smooth belly
over ebony bark
tongue tasting
corrupted air
languid body draped
over thick limbs.

You Are Not Who You Are

yellow spade leaves
drift down
stripping the tree
to a single
reptile.

Quadratic

Marie Hartung

3C is part one of an equation.
There is an equal sign somewhere.

Cancer is staged in numbers and letters
My wife's ovarian cancer is this part.

It's empty on the other side.

I read websites. Someone mentions 4B.
Another 1A. All math and incomplete words.

Add in statistics. 3C and 40% or maybe
20% if you also add b, r, c, and a.

Multiply by years or months expressed
as 30.5 or as in 5. Survival is quantified.

There are multiple answers which means
The solution isn't solvable.

Your God says it happened because
I didn't kneel and say my prayers.

Quadratic

Because I stole candy from the 7-11 in 4th grade.
Didn't finish catechism. Lied to my mom.

Didn't go to church—this church/that church.
Didn't read the Bible, the Qur'an, the scrolls.

I didn't do these things on a Tuesday,
every other Sunday, or holding hands at dinner.

Your God says bad things happen without belief.
That if I only accepted Jesus as my savior,

like a death row inmate, like a suicide bomber,
like a school shooter, like I'm supposed to.

Numbers are His punishment for an unfollowed
formula, for leaving off the equals and symbols.

The holy cross is a "t" which is no coincidence.

I pay my taxes, hug and kiss my children,
Never kill or maim a human or an animal.

But your God says I got it wrong.
Which is why I'm here with these letters,

trying to assign them numbers, so sure
that these odds are all quadratics. That we are.

Quadratic

I plug in: *I'm sorry, I'm sorry, I'm sorry*
to the other side of her 3C, to the long list

of variables in 46 years I didn't solve to His liking.
I factor the coefficient of the dead behind every digit.

Some rapist celebrates his 100th birthday
from a nursing home. 1/2/3/4.

Your God doesn't care. Differential equation.
Your God makes me carry the one.

My God says fuck off to yours.
It's better, I pencil, *to leave the logarithm empty.*

Executive Order:
Jerome County, Idaho

Susan Bruns Rowe

1918

You are standing in a grubbed-out desert. Behind you the land is flat and fades to a milky white in the distance. Two lonely fence posts live in that liminal space between land and sky. You are wearing white—that most impractical color. It's early days still. You've only just arrived from Texas where white was a shield against the sun. The sleeves on your dress have lace trim, and the bodice buttons in the back. How on earth did you ever put it on? A wide black sash around your waist separates your bottom and top halves. It is the only dark thing in the picture aside from your hair, a soft brown pulled high onto your head.

Off to the right, there is a small shack, an outhouse we might call it now, but I suspect you didn't call it that then. What is the German word for privy? What strikes me is your expression—the barest smile, not really a smile at all but more of an acquiescence. The photographer is your husband, and he is besotted with this new toy, so you agree to curve your lips because you love this man. Love him so much you followed him across the ocean and defied the aunt and uncle who raised you. He had not even offered to marry you, not then and not when you arrived in New York City. But that is another story.

Somewhere close by your children are playing. The sun is hot, glaring down, causing you to squint, but you are grateful it is dry, not the weight that smothered you in Texas, left you sick and exhausted. What will you do when this photo is snapped and your husband says something soft and mocking to you in German? Will you respond in kind? Will you lean in to kiss him and he you? Will you herd the children inside away from snakes and jackrabbits and the basalt cliffs on the edge of the Snake River Canyon and lay some sagebrush in the stove to light a fire and begin to cook a meal? And will you say a prayer for this barren desert that you now call home and for your young family and for all that you have come through and for all that lies ahead?

This was the picture you handed Mr. Smitt, the postmaster, on that hot July morning. You have traveled in the wagon pulled by the two Shires, Dolly and Jake. Your husband waits outside with the children. He is so bitter he could spit. Inside the small post office, around the corner from the ornate row of tiny metal doors that open to reveal empty boxes—you tell Mr. Smitt the purpose of your visit, and he nods and asks for your papers. You expect to be humiliated. You expect to be asked harsh questions. But Mr. Smitt asks only if you have any brothers or a father fighting in the war, and you tell him about your only sister married to an Italian taxi driver in New York. You tell him about your father, a coach driver in Osnabrück, and it's the first time you realize the odd coincidence that your sister has married a man with a profession like your father. But you hardly saw your father because he married again, had a second family, and you were sent to live with an aunt and uncle after your mother died. You think all this in the barest second but say only that you have no relatives who are enemy combatants, and Mr. Smitt nods and fills out the small gray booklet in his perfect penmanship. When it is your turn to sign on the line you try to match his beautiful handwriting or at least not mar this small book as your husband marred his. Then Mr. Smitt—Clarence is his first name and he writes his last with a lovely flourish over the double t's—asks if you have brought a photo, and you nod and hand him the one your husband took some months ago, on a Sunday afternoon. Very carefully, Mr. Smitt takes a small pot of glue and uses a brush to daub a thin coating on the back of the picture. Before he affixes it to the book, he makes sure it is perfectly centered, the top of the picture aligned with the top of a square box outlined in blue.

Then comes the moment you have been dreading and from Mr. Smitt's apologetic look, you know he has, too. He takes out a small ink pad and asks for your left hand. His hand is soft, not like your husband's calloused palm, and very gently he presses your thumb onto the ink and then onto the space below your newly mounted picture. There is an awkward silence while you wait for it to dry. Mr. Smitt picks the small book up and blows on it gently and for a moment you smell peppermint and beneath that, the eggs he had for breakfast. When he hands it to you he tells you to keep it with you at all times, and you nod your understanding and holding the little book that says you are an enemy alien who may be arrested and detained for the period of the war, you slide it into your purse and wonder how you will carry it while you dig a garden and mind your children and walk beside the horses while your husband guides the plow, and before you walk out the door, you touch your hand to your heart to stop it shaking.

1942

You are sitting on the edge of a bed, the chenille spread a touch of color in your tarpaper barracks. On one side your husband and on the other your mother-in-law with whom you share this small room. On your lap your baby daughter has a skin rash and your son, in your mother-in-law's lap, tugs his ear. You look at the camera, your lips slightly parted. Beside you, your handsome husband looks off at something in the cramped room framed by hanging laundry, suitcases stuffed beneath the bed, blankets piled on a chair. Your mother-in-law looks at the camera, too. Her lips are a closed line.

For the photo, you wear a skirt, your prettiest sweater, and dress the children in their best, too. Your shoes are practical, revealing slender ankles. The photographer is from the camp office, someone you do not know. Each flashbulb bursts, melts, then crackles leaving craters across the once smooth surface. You do not know what the picture is for or where it will appear. The children are getting restless and you cajole your son with the promise of a sweet from the camp store. You wonder where the photographers were when you packed up your home? Where are the pictures of the lush forests on the Sound, the ferns along the path leading to your front door, the tags you were instructed to wear and put on your children's coats, like bolts of fabric in a department store?

When the photographer leaves, you take off your sweater and undo the buttons on your blouse and help the baby latch. Your mother-in-law heats water for tea on the pot-belly stove. In a little while, you will all walk together to the canteen where you will sit beside strangers on benches and tables longer than a small ship and eat macaroni, spinach, beets. Now your husband paces the tiny room and smokes a cigarette. You wish he would go outside, but outside is row after row of barracks just like this one, and it rained last night, turning the dust to mud. Besides the guards in the tower would want to know why a man might pace back and forth like a tiger in the zoo. Your mother-in-law tells you your milk is too thin. That is why the baby's skin is red and papery. She rains down silent disapproval. It falls on you to knit this family together in this interminable internment, this interlude, and

Executive Order: Jerome County, Idaho

you give yourself to it, as you feed the baby with her hot skin, as you yield silently in the middle of the night to your husband, not wanting your mother-in-law to wake, not wanting, most of all, another child in this alien desert.

It is almost a relief when your husband is shipped out, a brave and loyal Nisei volunteering for his country, and you join the other women in the beet fields while his mother minds the children. And though you must stuff your blouse with an old dishcloth to stop your breasts from leaking through your clothes, you are grateful for the work. Grateful to be out of that tiny room where the children have no space to play and the single light bulb makes you want to shatter its weak incandescence with your shoe. You cannot understand why you are allowed only one when the photographer wasted so many.

This morning you ride with seven other women in the back of a farmer's pick-up truck to a field miles from camp. As the washboard road jars your body, you breathe in freshly cut hay and tie your scarf tighter beneath your chin. The farmer in his faded overalls is embarrassed. He demonstrates how to pull the beets and motions to the handcarts—he calls them wheelbarrows—used to gather the plants along the rows. At lunchtime, his wife brings a tray of sandwiches and you sit beneath the shade of a poplar tree, its gnarled trunk gray with age, and listen to the laughter of the unmarried girls. You sit with the other mothers and middle-aged and eat in silence.

Now you use your fingers to reach deep into the loamy soil sprung from ancient volcanoes that covered this sagebrush plateau millions of years before you arrived on the train and then bus with your young family and the possessions you could carry. You plant your feet, use both hands, pull from the base where the leafy stem meets the white meat. The sugar beet root is long and slender and feeds the white, tear-shaped tuber. You no longer hope for an end to the war. You no longer hope to return to the home you once had. You hope only to hold your children at the end of each day, to smell the sweet smell of them. You hope the lone lightbulb burns long enough to sketch in your notebook when they go to sleep. You hope your husband comes home alive. You hope when you are an old woman bitterness will not be your mask.

2017
You are standing in the milking parlor with your back to the camera. One hand touches the cow's flank, the other grasps the tangle of metal tubes and rubber hoses that hangs from a chain above you. You wear latex gloves and a plastic apron over your hoodie. You have agreed to the picture on condition the photographer not show your face. Only your smooth cheek is visible and your long brown hair pulled back into a messy bun.

You have been up since three this morning, rolling from your boyfriend's bed to stumble into your jeans and rubber boots in the dark. He does not even wake when you open the door and a burst of desert wind knifes around the corner before you slip out, locking the door behind you. The woman taking pictures for the magazine is impressed by the gleaming lunchroom, the row of metal lockers, clean restrooms and showers. There is even a supply of Kotex on the counter. Your mother has worked in dairies where there was only a single plastic porta-potty outside, where the workers twisted the cows' tails when they refused to move, twisted them until the bone cracked and the tail hung limp so each time the cow defecated, it shit all over itself.

The owner walks through to check the line, but the cows know the routine which they practice three times a day. He is telling the

Executive Order: Jerome County, Idaho

woman from the magazine how the dairy business can't exist without illegals. His son was in your class at high school and you helped him pass geometry. When you see him around the dairy, you remember him shy and pimpled back then. But that was a long time ago, before you began working for his father for fourteen dollars an hour. You tried college for a while, but even with your scholarship, you couldn't afford it, and you knew better than to apply for aid. All that paperwork, the forms you had to fill out, it made your mother nervous. She said it would get you both deported, and that is why you moved out. When you see her at Mass on Sundays she is always hassling you, telling you birth control is a sin. You say bringing a child into the world, that would be a sin.

Everyone knows someone who has been deported. A few weeks ago you asked the owner if you could work in the office, do the bookkeeping. He shook his head, seemed genuinely sorry. If his banker found out, there could be a raid and he can't take the risk. So each day, you slide from bed in the blue dark, pull your glossy hair back, and wear the same jeans three days in a row before the stink of manure and rotten milk is more than you can stomach and you must tote your clothes to the laundromat two blocks down from the apartment.

When your 12-hour shift ends, you catch a ride home, shower and change. Your boyfriend is at work and you like it that way, these hours to be alone. You set out, walking past St. Catherine's Church, the lava rock stones cut by the Basques and Irish whose children and grandchildren now work at the courthouse and the hospital. It has not rained for three months, and the dust leaves a fine coating on your ankles in the space between your jeans and sneakers. You walk for another mile on the gravel road to the Benedictine monastery on a hill above the dairies and hay fields. There you take communion with the aging monks who call you by name as they place the Host in the palm of your hand and hold the cup for you to drink. You light a candle and silently say the prayer you offer every time you come. When you start home the sky is a heart-breaking shade of blue with floating cities of white clouds. The desert wind pushes against you, bringing with it the smell of the dairy so you can never forget what you do and who you are. You stop beside a small wood of poplar and pine some far-sighted monk planted years ago. Above the trees and power lines, four red-tailed hawks soar, hovering on the wind. They float effortlessly, not moving their wings, suspended above the plowed stubble and rows of corn, above the tick of sprinklers arcing silver streams onto the cracked earth. They fly in place, held by forces not their own, in a kind of limbo between earth and sky. You stand fascinated and watch. You watch them so long the blood-orange sun touches down on the horizon before you. Still you stand and watch. You stand and watch until the first star and its pale moon appear. You cannot tear your eyes away.

If You Could Tell Your Story with Wings

Madronna Holden

If you could tell your story with wings
my sky would be larger
than it is now

(Though the mountains
would still know how
to find us.)

A story like that would warm us
in our nest until we peered
over the edge and fell
into flying

Such a story would
make everything count
as we passed among
the otherwise
unnumbered stars

If You Could Tell Your Story with Wings

Make everything
more than imagination
as it gathered us
into its words

Then we wouldn't be
stumbling, but practicing
on the runway
of the sky

We wouldn't be crying
but bringing rain
to the land.

One June Day: Fire, Heat, and Children Locked in Cages at the Texas-Mexico Border

Nancy Flynn

here
in this land of savagery & lies,
a spider's net between a branch & the eucalyptus chair

jails a brittle,
falling leaf
where,

on my island of dawning
bells, the horns are just disappearing
freight & the gutters need to be cleaned of more

fallen, the falling
broken
but still

here
as the trees reach
out for a sky turned scorch

One June Day

yet more gasping, bitter
smoke at a sunrise that blinds, ashes
our eyes to the sight

of the cruelties while prop
planes overhead deaden the pitch,
every cry

Straw, Sticks, & Brick

John Sibley Williams

Blow down: submit to: every now & then

along the orchard's edge a wolf
 in wolf's clothing

& we say in our hearts *come, please come closer*

while shouting for all we're worth
 we're worth more

than another's nourishment: both pleas as true
as we can make them, which is to say sometimes

with our house at its sturdiest we embrace ruin

to restore what we forgot we have: which is why half the people

 I love voted for fear, which is why fear like
 love keeps us on our toes:

which is to say we trust the brick house will endure again, which is
    not to say
    it will,

but as we all must trust in something, I'm saying I get it: trust the sky

will burn as brilliantly after it closes   its jaws around us

    & we let it swallow.

Zum Wohl
—*for Stephanie Mueller Andrade*

Christine DeSimone

"My party fell in the water," my deaf German friend says,
translating *ein schlag ins wasser* as if from
a book of verse in her hands.
"Did I say that right?"

She means that no one showed.
She doesn't mind, nor does she hear,
the thunk of cork
unplugged from its wine. Her voice

is a gurgle from a water pipe
and her words burst like a golden memory.
She laughs at everything, fermenting
an uncharted sound. She was eleven

when Chernobyl's cloud drifted to Stuttgart
and spilled a halo of hair chunks onto her pillow.
For a year she couldn't play in the rain,
so she window-watched the poison

Zum Wohl

mist on morning grassblades,
each dewdrop a deadly, pulsing grape.
The boy next door, not so lucky, aged and curdled
until he was smothered by his own white blood cells.

I wonder if language really does what it says it does.
So many events happen silently. *Zum wohl*, she says,
clinking her glass to mine and surveying the empty room.
Above us, the simple soft hum of evening stars.

Mud

Hollyn Taylor

Franka has just finished filling the dented kettle with fresh water and placing it on the boiler. She turns the range dial to the hottest setting and listens to the click-whoosh of the stove's flame coming to life. While Franka waits for the water to roll and boil, she walks over to the window that overlooks her jungled, unkempt front yard. With the tip of her fingernail, she gently raises a slat in the blinds and peeks out.

Beyond her front door a savanna lay at her porch filled with molten sands of screaming hyenas and a blood-scented sunrise. Out there—*beyond*—awaits a dizzying heatstroke from exposure to the elements of human experience.

trees branches nest holding eggs held together by earth dried hard in westward sunshine; fall to the ground little bloody yolks pan sizzling cracking popping popping popping; dead baby bird little fledgling whose feet never held a branch a berry fermented in winter like bees stuck in sap.

Franka eyes the clock, the seconds dripping off its heavy arms.

The school buses will be coming soon.

From behind the safety of her dusty cobweb-crackled window, Franka keeps watch as an armada of sun-golden buses dock against the curbs of cemented ports. She's lulled by the ebb and flow of the tide, by the waves of children disembarking from metal vessels and scuttling to dry land. She watches the tide bring change, as they shed sea-legs from their bodies before they lope from the shore, through the tall, sky-reaching grasses, and across the rivers of pebble-chipped cement.

It's only when Franka sees the boy that she allows the air to deflate from her nervous lungs, the vortices of breath shaking the branches of her anxious capillaries. She watches the little boy with the comet-trail arms, the boy who always waits longer than everyone else for his someone to come get him. She gazes at his star-kissed skin and his giant Jupiter eyes—eyes that glitter in his skull like cracked marbles steeped in saltwater.

glacial erratics lurch through eons footprints carve canyons; muddied roads feet slick slip slide over asphalt like snowmelt; tinier hands on tiny faces smiling cheery-eyed chipped-toothed happy happy happy waiting for their rides; alley cats slinking climbing running cunning; wisteria dancing wind sonata zephyrs cut through dusk; knife-slick teeth bite cartilage snap burst air lungs popped like fat grub in peckish beaks of birds; back to the nest back to the nest back to the nest.

The clock ticks over.

The kettle screams.

It's been a wet spring. Everything's waterlogged or covered with the silty muck of rainfall and algae bloom. In the evening, the cricketed twilight marches in moments to the percussion of the glittering sidereal timelessness.

There's new life out there. Sapling dryads stretch their eager infant roots into rich black soils. Coyotes are mantled in their nightfurs and, during the bluest hours of the night, Franka can hear their pups skipping through empty fields and farmlands—terrorizing weasels, chickens, cats.

Mud

There's new desire out there. Lovers in their bedroom washed in embrace, kissing sparks on moon-blushed skin with the lips of young blind love. Their widened, silent, laugh-love smiles mock all the bad days that haven't found their new address. Franka, mantled in the night, voyeurs behind her vine-veiled window. Her lips rush red, her pupils hold lakes.

longing blood salted breath taste of human taste adrenaline paramour inamorata; copper pennies batteries touching tongues; mineral locked in lakes hold rocks sink lead locked in ice; seed pit roots waiting to break free patience patience patience; frozen fox in winter tundra melting; infertile human touch dirt-sick blight watered acid rain; blood-flushed heart-knocking drunkenness ten billion leaded butterflies clunking sinking down; empty stomachs mouths minds; sink down like bees stuck in sap.

Franka spots the boy before he leaves the bus. She watches him linger in the back, determined to be the last one to step off. She often wonders which days he'll be picked up, and which days he'll be forgotten. Some days, he's not there at all. Then there are the days when he stares down the road and, whenever he spots a familiar car, looks like a love-starved dog on a sun-stained sidewalk waiting for his master.

Kindred.

He walks from the school bus, sits at the bus stop, and stares down at his feet. He looks angry, he looks sad. He kicks the dirt and spits on the ground. His head hangs lower and all the small branches of his body wilt from the drought-sick soil where he first took root.

Franka remembers being that small, confused, and abandoned. She remembers hiding inside her classrooms during recesses on the years' coldest days—ruining her teachers' lunch breaks. She would stand against the finger-greased windows and stroke the cold metal latches, feeling the sharp edges strum against her fingerprints. She'd stand and stare out at the school yard, her tiny panicked breath giving birth to cities of clouds on the glass.

She remembers being that little girl, stuck inside, desperately wanting to go home to a place that was safer than where she was. She remembers how badly she wanted to run, to break through the door and race against the wind. How desperately she needed to be pulled from the tar of her own brain chemistry.

what's wrong with you; are you broken(?) are you broken(!) are you broken(?!) point and laugh; hold my breath hold it in; it stays with me it stays with me it stays with me; holding pulsing skipping heart-beaten; sticky-skinned moon-faced waning; skies sparkling down on lake-tops fishlike hungry mouths grope; floated bloated pollen sprigs fronds descend to lake-beds drowned like bees stuck in sap.

With her memories pounding in her heart, she leaves the kettle on the stove and paces to her room. In the doorway, she grips the edge of the frame. Her fingernails dig into the wood, and bits of paint poke at the soft pink skin under her nails. She begins to count backward, waiting for her feet to stop floating, waiting for the static behind her eyes to discharge.

She breaks from the doorway and smashes a button on her stereo. She listens as the music begins to leak out. She sits on her bed, presses her eyes closed, and retreats deeper into her mental panic room. She tries to remember how to breathe. She works to match the rise and fall of her chest with the crescendo of the trumpets, a soundtrack for the world within her world.

She sits, her mind orbiting at light speed. She listens to her breathing, waiting for those screaming kids to go home—waiting for the trumpets to take them, to take their voices and carry them up into the sky, through the clouds, and across the meandering currents of air and out into the oceans of atmosphere.

Focus.

Breathe.

the trees the river the shores the lakes let the lakes swallow the trees rushing river sloshing water on rocks; bubbling belching silt sediment drowned fawn in the icy spring water hoof caught in rocks; trees holding branches drowned with leaves; fermented berries drunken robins fall fall fall to the ground like bees stuck in sap.

A metal-burn vapor seeps into the room and patches the chasm Franka fissured in her mind, fusing her back to reality. The sweet-bile acidity in the air stings her nostrils and stains the back of her throat.

Metal on fire.

Her head spins her body around and she flies to the kitchen. On the stove, small flames kiss thick, black, powdery streaks across the base of the kettle.

Franka re-readies the base-burnt kettle with fresh water, places it on the stovetop, and turns the dial back up to high. She walks across the kitchen and peeks out the window, spying through the narrow metal slats.

She watches.

Franka's daydreams dissolve when the sound of breaking glass tears through her eardrums. She jolts to the sound and knocks up against the corner of the countertop. She winces as she steps away from the formica and places a hand on her hip as if she were trying to stop a wound from bleeding.

She walks toward the front of her house and there, in the living room, lying on the floor, is a crumpled ball of feathers amongst the sharp, scattered, shimmering geometry of her broken window.

bird through the window pin-needle plumage; hawk through window chasing waxwings; he got away he got away he got away; he lead her to her death broke her neck; small blood leaked down a beak broken half off; broke her neck broke the window shrieked in shattered splinters; culling of birds birth of spring printemps primavera; plushdowny shrike-kin died in the dirt little skeletons; it died in here it died in here it died in here.

Today is the day that the boy gets tired of waiting for whomever it was that wasn't coming to get him. With boiling blood, he rises with a furious steam that furrows his brows and presses an angry scowl into his metaled face.

Today is the day he decides to go through a neighboring yard and cut through the empty, naked land that grieved its razed groves generations ago.

Franka crosses her kitchen to the window that looks out over her weed-reclaimed back yard. She surveys the tousled property. She watches a murmuration of starlings swoop and dip and dive as one fluid movement—spilled like ink across the scroll of the horizon. She sees the ink drip from their wings and fall to the ground as rain.

The boy trudges through the murky morass and Franka can almost hear the *thuck-thucking* of his boots with each step. He takes one more step and the earth decides it's keeping his shoe. Her breath breaks along with her disassociation. She holds the air between her fingertips like the pages of some precious pristine parchment.

Breathe.

Mud

fold pages blithely gingerly softly softly softly; codex incunabulum vade mecum hold edges prickled torn tattered border; kiss the ripples of fingertips pressing invisible ink-blots into fingerprints; hold me catch me in folds turns creases; fiber that will live until a fire spits out ash and falls to the ground like bees stuck in sap.

She watches the boy with a fixed laser-gaze as wisps of peppermint and ginger kiss her corneas. She sips her tea.

She watches him hurl his bag and shout to the ground, muddying the dirt with his small angry tears. She watches as his knees collapse from under him and he drops to the ground like a wet rag.

She watches as his fists begin beating the sticky muck.

She watches as he sinks and slumps—broken.

The rain stampedes him. It pushes him down and pounds against his skull. Little palm-shaped pools form at his wrists and knees. He looks up at the sky and he can do nothing but stare—his face twisted with a look only a forgotten child wears.

She watches as he tries to stand and pull his foot from the mud but the lonely, codependent clay clings tight and resists the separation.

Franka knows if she stops watching then the boy will free himself. He'll rise and run, barefoot, through the rest of the flooding fen. She knows he'll arrive home and be greeted with warm embraces and a hot bath by the people who love him and have been worried about where he's been. She knows if she turns now—right now—and goes back to the kitchen for more tea, the rain will stop and no flash floods will fill the valley.

But Franka does not stop watching the boy, her breathing staggered and shallow. Shallower than the water filling the pit the boy has dug around himself, shallower than the now-tepid water sitting peacefully at the bottom of the old burnt kettle on the stove.

Lightning flays the sky, and thunder sends shivers into the teacups in Franka's cupboard.

She watches.

The boy's movements are slowing, his face still twisted with anger—but there's more fear now than rage.

She watches as he slouches his body to the side and curls up in the mud-womb he's carved for himself.

She watches hope rise off his body like steam.

The kettle begins to whistle.

When the water reaches its boiling point—when its dancing atoms have gained enough energetic momentum, they break from the molecular manacles of their liquid prisons and escape as vapor into the air.

When the boy's movements stop altogether, Franka shouts with a voice that no one can hear and drops the teacup from her hands. It smashes on the hardwood and bits of painted porcelain spray out carelessly across the floor.

She rushes to the sliding door and presses her palms against the window. The door has always been locked, but Franka notices her fingers reaching for the latch.

The kettle screams.

She pries open the door and its rusted track scratches as the slider drags across the moss-coated frame. The wind kicks her in the teeth. The earth quakes from the echoes of the heartbeats of all her dead ancestors. Her throat constricts.

little baby bird hold tight hold tight hold tight to branches frozen solid; false spring chill to the bone fell to the ground like a bee stuck in sap.

Barefoot, she steps over the threshold and sets foot on Saturn—the earth more alien than anything she's ever felt—the grass blades prickling the soles of her tender feet. The rain falls on her, adorning her body with liquid light and gemstones. The raindrops roll down her trauma-tattooed skin—down her arms, her knuckles, her nails. Steaming droplets of skin-salted rainwater, boiled by the blaze of her churning blood, drip from her shaking fingertips and fall to the ground like bees stuck in sap.

Where Lovers Meet

Diane Averill

They hide inside a rhododendron flower,
let it bloom around their nude bodies,
unseen.

Sometimes they meet in a treehouse,
make love by flashlight at night,
staying way past moon time.

The prudish might look for them,
but the lovers can change form
and squirrel up the pines.

Anyone can hear their love
in the cries of birds,
or the sounds of crickets at magic hour,

but these are ubiquitous.
You can try following the creek,
and they might be there,

but they will dive into their own currents,
rivering their way down stream
quick as minnows.

Some weave blankets from maple leaves,
use tulip petals for pillows soft as caresses,
or if in danger, slip into a fern, and uncurl their tips.

If you tend to condemn,
look way back to that young version
of your lost joy, and tiptoe quietly away.

The Man Who Cuts My Hair

Peter Serchuk

The man who cuts my hair has heard it all:
From high and low, the best and worst,
from every perch, up and down, on the ladder.
So each month, for an hour, I hear about the lives
of other men: tales of brokers, actors, lawyers
and accountants. And I'd be lying if I said I didn't listen.
Scissors snapping in my ears like castanets, I learn about
the one who struck it rich then bought a curvy, younger wife.
The one who rigged the books and now reads inside a cell.
The one who lived to eat until an artery blew a fuse.
Still, as he cuts and trims, shaves and clips, I can't help
but wonder what tales he tells when others take my place.
About a guy who fell asleep in the bridle of convention?
Or some lucky fool with the Midas touch?
Maybe some middle-aged hipster too eager to embrace
an earring and tattoo. The list goes on and on,
the possibilities endless. My head now spinning in a dream,
I see them all, wearing my clothes, crowding the mirror.
There's something familiar in the way each one bobs and weaves.
Then I'm back in the room, eyebrows being trimmed,
watching him, the man who cuts my hair, clean my neck
and lower my chair. I stand and pay his fee.

The Man Who Cuts My Hair

"You look like a million bucks," he says.

I stare into the mirror of his eyes, tip him an extra twenty.

He slaps my back and shakes my hand, as if he knows me.

A Question of Time

Tara K. Shepersky

Every time he leaves, I hear his death.

This morning while my consciousness nudged his
and they agreed just five more minutes,
I imagined the phone call.
And I thought I'd better start now,
kissing him goodbye.

The last one shared
beneath wildfire skies
in this latest hottest summer.

This morning particulate levels
went red again, which is 'stay inside.'
Imagine this seriously.
My city is taking trophies for pollution
and we pray for wind. I conjure his

breath.
Another
endangered species.

A Question of Time

At afternoon, the long-desired shift.
The scent of rain arriving
is the rattle of my beloved's key
in the lock of the long-parched house.
But he's not returned.

Don't you imagine
that I would rather
be wrong?

Then he's there to kiss my forehead
and my breath restarts. Tomorrow is
September, middle age, 8 billion humans.
I am not burning, today.
But always: the smoke.

Strangers

*—After William Stafford's "Easter Morning,"
with a borrowed opening*

Matthew J. Spireng

Maybe someone comes to the door and says,
"Repent," and you think if you are to be saved
you need to be as you came into this world,

so you say, "Hold on a minute," and you go
to your bedroom where you remove your clothes,
all your clothes, and return to the door, where

two strangers are waiting, and you invite the strangers in,
offer coffee or soft drinks and discuss whatever
the strangers want, which is not your nakedness.

In fact, the strangers seem to only be interested in
converting you to their faith. If it were *your* faith,
the strangers would have run from your door

the moment you reappeared, naked and welcoming,
offering coffee or soft drinks, and acting as if
nothing at all was the least bit strange.

Eureka

LaVonne Griffin-Valade

I kid you not, I once knew a guy named Red Black.

In the late forties, I signed on with a timber-falling outfit in Northern California, and Red was the crew boss. He was an intimidating presence—thick, hard arms, a boxer's broad chest, and solid as a granite cliff. Years before I met him, he'd been ejected through the windshield of a buddy's Nash Ambassador. He fared the accident pretty well except for his nose, half of which clung to the other half by a thread of bloody tissue. They'd managed to repair it, but he was left with a scarred-over rift running from tear duct to nostril on one side of his face.

Most of us on the falling crew had been to the war or were too old to have gone in the first place. Others had flat feet or problems with an alimentary canal, irregularities that got you classified as 4-F and unfit for military service. With the war behind us, we were all just workingmen and mainly glad of it. But by the time Friday afternoons rolled around, we were usually sick to death of soggy weather and the reek of rain forest with its noxious scent of rotting vegetation, an odor almost worse than anything I'd smelled at the Battle of Saipan.

At quitting time one particular Friday, Red's deep, amplified voice called for a hasty departure. "Move your asses, girls. I'm meeting my lady friend at The Whiskey Trot, and I ain't going to be late because of your goddamned dawdling."

We piled into the crummy soon enough, and Red got behind the wheel. The rest of us claimed seats and sprawled out for napping purposes on the drive back to Eureka.

Red let the engine warm, flipped on the windshield wipers, rearranged his jacket, and poured himself some coffee from the Thermos sitting on the dashboard. The rhythm of the idling crummy and rain slapping against our windows was strangely soothing and would have eased me toward sleep, had Red not shut off the engine.

"What the hell is that?" he said.

Some of the men in the back didn't hear the question or were already dozing, but those of us sitting up front started rubbernecking, trying to figure out what would cause Red to leave off heading back to town.

He pulled the handle, opened the door, and moved down the steps. One by one, the whole crew filed wearily out of the crummy behind him and into the early autumn deluge, even the men who'd been lazing in the back.

Red pointed toward a stand of Douglas fir. "Christ on a crutch. What is that?"

A silvery contraption hovered about a hundred feet above the treetops. Except for the steady downpour and the creak of the crummy settling back into wet earth, nothing made a sound, not even the ravens or the turkey buzzards.

Two of the three men who'd fought in the European theater quietly speculated it was some kind of dirigible or a blimp, maybe even a zeppelin.

The third man, Norbert, said it was definitely no such thing. "First of all there's no basket hanging from the belly. Plus, the outside's made of some kind of metal."

"How can you tell that from here?" Red asked.

"Well, I can't be sure without binoculars, I s'pose. But just look at it," Norbert said. "The way it shimmers against the clouds."

We stood together, gawking up at the curious orb, some snickering and some sighing tiredly. A patch of sun, its light fiercely angled, fell across the tattered earth and struck our mud-caked contingent.

"I've heard about this kind of thing before," Everett said.

Ev had a wooden leg on account of some logging accident back before the war, but he knew how to keep his balance and always managed his end of a two-man chainsaw. "It's what they call an unidentified flying object. UFO for short."

"You mean a flying saucer?" the kid Hank asked. "How come it ain't shaped like a dish then?"

"Don't know," Ev said, "but there it is."

"What's it doing here?" I asked.

Ev just shrugged.

"Red, I got my pistol in the crummy," Corbin offered.

Red smirked. "To do what with?"

"S'pose it lands and some Jerrys or Japs get out? Start shootin, I don't know."

"War's been over for a few years now, you know that Corbin," Red said.

"S'pose they don't know the war's over? Such things has happened."

Corbin was the only one of us to ever challenge Red's way of seeing things, but it always came with a price, usually in the form of tougher work duties. It was hard to watch, Corbin being over forty-five and closer to being old than the rest of us. He'd be stuck falling one tree after another while standing at a near vertical incline at the top of some ridge, whether or not the rain poured down brutal and relentless, and all on account of Red's peeved-off disposition.

"Or s'pose it's the Ruskies?"

"Stop flapping your lips, Corbin."

Red gave the man one of his scar-faced scowls. That's when it came to me for the first time that his hair wasn't red like you'd expect when a person's called such. It was his face that had taken on a deep shade of crimson.

Corbin, in disgust, took off his hardhat and reboarded the crummy.

After a good twenty minutes, the luminous, slightly elongated, oval-like wonder moved directly overhead and disappeared into the cloud mass. As quickly though, it was back, this time lower in the sky and hanging above us. As it moved closer in and hovered, I thought I heard the crepitating sound of radio waves fading in and out, crackling through the air. Shortly, it lifted and abruptly flew off.

As we climbed back on the crummy, Red pulled his bottle of hooch from the glove box and took a great swig. He scratched his chin whiskers with an index finger and offered the jug to each of us, including the boy Hank.

"Corbin! Get your ass up here. I got Sonny Brook," Red called to the back.

Corbin edged up to the front and took his hit of warm whiskey.

Red lifted the bottle and toasted the seven members of his crew. "Cheers, girls. Can't say nothing about this to nobody back in Eureka, though. Understood?"

The rest of us gave one another a knowing look. Meaning we knew Red. Even though he'd not fought in the war and never even been a military man, he always handed out orders like he had.

"Don't you see it? We'd be taken for fools. Too unreliable to hire."

We all nodded, mostly so we could finally get on the road.

Red took another swig. "I remember stuff like this from the Depression, working down in Modesto where there's nothing but dust and piped-in water. Some of you've been there, so you know what I mean. People spot this fucking flying saucer shit all the time down in Modesto."

He twisted on the cap and put the bottle of hooch back in the glove box. "Some asshole took a picture once. Bunch of stupid shits bought it too. Turned out to be an old hubcap the asshole had flung up in the air."

That night after our gyppo logging crew drove back to Eureka and scattered to our separate trailer houses, rented rooms, and tenant shacks—or in Red Black's case, his long-time lady friend's boarding house—I told Stanette about the silver machine we'd seen hovering above the treetops.

Stanette was a nice girl. Shy. Slender. I was thinking we might get married sometime.

"Hovering, huh?" she said, picking at her chicken-fried steak. "Like a hot air balloon or something?"

Sometimes I wondered if she had trouble with the way I looked—the dishwater blonde hair, the horned nose, and the crop of brown moles along my chin. She always cast her eyes to the floor or her lap when talking to me.

"No, not a balloon or a blimp, or anything like that. Wasn't like anything any of us has ever seen," I said, swallowing chunks of meatloaf pie. "Awful pretty the way it glowed and hung there for a while then came in closer. Like the thing was watching us or something."

"Why would it be watching you boys?"

"Don't know it was for sure. We were probably more curious about it than the other way around." I washed down the rest of my meatloaf pie with cold iced tea. "Ev says it was a UFO."

"A what?"

"Means unidentified flying object. Red told us not to say anything about it."

"Red's a smart guy, you ask me. No need getting folks stirred up, thinking there's something weird flying around out there."

"He was more worried people would think we're all nuts."

"Shoot, it's probably just some secret military thing. Like the A-bomb."

We finished up our supper at the little diner on Highway 101, and I walked Stanette back to her mother's house. For a change, I wasn't circling the talk around the moment at the front steps when I would lean in and kiss her. Seemed I'd momentarily lost my enthusiasm for it.

Later in my room at the Humboldt Motel, I thought of what Stanette had said about that UFO. She couldn't of got that right. What us men saw out in the forest, glimmering against the clouds was nothing the military could build. World War II had taught me that much.

Lying stiff and hemmed-in on my small cot, I had a hard time going to sleep. I finally dozed, but woke up with the sweats. I heard a low crackling somewhere in the room. Damn mice, I thought. Or worse, wood rats. The motel was famous for its giant ones. The sound got some louder. I sat up, turned on the floor lamp resting beside my cot.

"Hello? Someone there?"

I cleared my throat and sat in the otherwise dark room waiting for what might come next, even if it was just a visit from wood rats.

"Hello?" I said again.

Finally I turned off the light and lay back on the cot. The crackling had stopped.

I dreamt I was on day six at my guard post on Saipan. Just across the channel, I saw the Enola Gay lifting off from Tinian, the big super bomber arcing heavily under its load, flying out over the Pacific in a long black shadow, delivering the A-bomb to its target. I saw the shining burst, the blast, brighter than that silver orb sailing above the treetops.

I woke up sweating again. But this time I knew it was because of the dream. In real life, witnessing the obliteration of Hiroshima would've been impossible. Saipan and Tinian being 1500 miles from Japan.

Next morning, the boy Hank knocked at my motel room. I slipped on my pants, opened the door, and signaled him to come inside.

"Hey, Dale. Ain't supposed to rain today. Let's go hunt mushrooms."

This was the first I'd heard anything about mushrooms. "I need coffee, Hank. Let's go get breakfast at the diner first."

"Ma already made me breakfast."

"I don't have a ma for that."

"Well, we gotta get out there early if we're gonna beat the other foragers."

Hank had the red hair Red didn't, and he was a scrawny thing with purple lips and a high forehead. You could see signs of being marked by small pox if you looked close enough. But he was no trouble on the crew, and we all liked him fine.

"We'd be hunting mushrooms in the woods, right?"

"Yeah," he said.

"Why would I want to go back out to the woods on my Saturday?"

"For Chanterelles. They're the best. 'Course what if that thing we saw yesterday's out there?"

I was already walking to the lavatory in my faller's pants, cut off at mid-shin and held up with suspenders. I didn't answer the kid.

At the diner on Highway 101, I wolfed down my breakfast while Hank listed off the particulars of a Tarzan film he'd recently seen at the Orpheum Theater. Half listening, I checked out the *Times-Standard* someone had left on the table, searching for news of a UFO sighting.

"Were you afraid watching that flying saucer yesterday?" I asked.

"Red said not to talk about it," Hank whispered and checked out the all-but-empty diner for listeners.

"You were the one who brought it up earlier. Besides, I'm not talking about anything you didn't see with your own eyes."

"I was a little scared I guess."

"Did you tell your ma about it last night?"

"Gosh no. I'd never tell my ma nothin about that. She'd be upset, and I wouldn't get to go to the woods and look for mushrooms." He paused and eyed my plate. "Are you about done with your breakfast? We gotta get goin."

We walked to Hank's house, and I waited on the stoop while he went inside to haggle with his ma for car keys. Overhead the sun burned through the lingering fog and left a shimmer of clear light from Eureka proper down to the ocean.

I stared up at the pierce of blue sky, searching for a flash of silver. "Where the hell are you?"

"Right here," Hank said. "We're taking my ma's old tan coupe parked in the carport."

Hank helped me figure out what a Chanterelle was so I wouldn't pick anything poisonous. Then we walked deep into tall timber where it was thick with shade and rich with nurse logs.

"This is the best place to find em," he said.

He was right. There were so many of the stinky golden things among the redwood and cedar, it took us a few hours to pick over the three or four good patches.

Finally, our flour sacks full, we came to an open swath of clear-cut forest. Immense stumps and huckleberry, a few live oak and vine maple, some snags and salal lay in our path. Bright daylight poured over the tortured Earth, the detritus of an enormous logging operation.

We hefted ourselves onto the remains of a giant redwood and sat. Hank peeled off his rucksack and drew out his lunch. He shared his Thermos of lukewarm Ovaltine and handed me one of the two beef-hash sandwiches his ma had bagged up for him.

"Thanks, but I bet your ma intended both of those sandwiches for you."

"She don't have to know. Now eat up."

They smelled so good I didn't need much convincing, and after our little picnic, I lay back on the Redwood stump, rolled up my jacket, and used it for a pillow.

When I yanked awake, Hank had gone off somewhere, leaving our sacks of Chanterelles tucked in the shade of an enormous slash pile. I sat up and tried to gauge the cardinal directions, like I'd learned in the Marines. But for studying practical things like orienteering and such, I would've had no fondness for my time as a Jarhead at all.

Some men felt guilty for not making it to the war. Maybe I was nothing but a coward, but I wished I'd never been part of it—the stench, the heat, the noise, all that blood. No one else knew this about me, not even Stanette. Fact was, she didn't know much about me, and now that I thought about it, didn't seem interested in knowing much.

During the Battle of Saipan, I'd killed the only Japanese soldier I ever knowingly killed. Shot him at the foot of Mt. Topatchau. Just a boy really, alone and scared shitless like me. I could still remember the look of surprise on his dying face.

I didn't like thinking about the dead Japanese boy, so I willed myself to remember yesterday's UFO. And before I could even begin hoping it would somehow materialize, the metallic contraption eased across the sky. Further away this time, but like before, brilliant and radiant among the clouds. That it was moving so quickly and in the opposite direction made me anxious.

I jumped from the redwood stump and called out, "Here! Over here!"

Ambling forward, I pulled myself over slash heaps, around stumps and rotting snags, across the blighted and logged-over land. I stopped, raised my arms above my head, and waved my whole body back and forth.

"Hey! Over here! Over here!" I cried, my voice echoing from the steep hills beyond. But the enigmatic airship slipped through the clouds and out of sight.

On my way back to the stump, I was surprised to see Red Black's crummy parked at the end of the logging road next to the clear cut, not to mention spotting the man himself strolling toward me.

"Dale?" he said. "What the hell are you doing here?"

"Hunting mushrooms with Hank." I pointed to the bulging flour sacks placed beside the slash pile.

"You like them smelly things?"

I fiddled with an earlobe and shrugged. "So what brings you out here?"

"I come to see about our next job." He looked me up and down. "Reminds me, why're you in your faller's gear on the weekend?"

I sunk my hands in the pockets of my raggedy, shin-length dungarees. "It's about all the clothes I own."

"Guess that explains why you're living in a shabby motel, huh? That's why I hate the goddamned military," Red went on in the righteous manner I often found irritating. "They send you off to war, and when you come home and go back to civilian life, you gotta fucking fend for yourself."

"Well, I'm hoping to save a little, maybe use the GI Bill to move myself up a notch or two."

"The government don't want your kind moving up a notch or two."

"My kind?"

"Poor white trash."

I wanted to punch Red in his red face. It wasn't only his meanness—that was just part of the package—it was his need to go after a fellow, find your tender spot and keep pressing and pressing until you liked to die.

But as usual, I didn't have a smart comeback to his insult.

I climbed back on the stump and sat down. "Did you see it?"

"Did I see what?"

"That UFO from yesterday." I pointed at it now flying slowly off to the left.

It stopped, floated, and then shifted closer. I was thrilled to see the gleaming craft move toward us, was sure I could hear the crackling noise.

I lay back, rested my head on my makeshift pillow. The silvery contrivance edged in just overhead, lighting and warming me. I closed my eyes. The air sizzled, turned heavy and dank. A prickling charge of energy rolled over my body.

I was inexplicably overcome with joy. Not joy exactly, more akin to contentment, something I hadn't felt since I was a kid like Hank, living with a ma who made sure I got my breakfast.

It was as if the war never happened, and I'd never killed that boy soldier, and the A-bomb had been a nightmare and nothing more.

I feared I would cry with Red standing right there. I pressed my rough, blistered hands over my eyes to shut down the burst of old, held-back tears and listened to the thrum of my heart.

After several minutes, I sensed the UFO moving off silently. I sat up and watched it disappear.

I didn't know what to think about what had just happened. Was the orb a message from God, a voyager from another world, a top-secret military experiment? All I knew was I was alive and a weight had been lifted somehow.

Standing up on the stump, I turned slowly and took in the expansive clear-cut mountainside. Where was Red, I wondered? I searched for his crummy. It too had vanished.

"Here I am Dale! I heard you yelling!" Hank tracked through the forest litter. He carried another flour sack, holding it as if the contents were precious gems.

With the heel of my palm, I wiped the tears and streaks of sweat. I cleared my throat. "More Chanterelles?"

"Nah, morels this time." He gave off one of his toothy grins. "Lots of em along the edge of the clear cut."

Myself, I barely knew a Chanterelle from a warty tree burl, and I had no interest in his sack full of whatevers, but I believed I knew just what to say. "Your ma will be plumb excited about all those shrooms."

"She will for sure. Got enough for Red and all the men, too. We'll be heroes."

"Speaking of Red, did you see him?" I asked.

Hank gazed back over the acres of stumps and snags. "Red was here?"

"Just a few minutes ago. And the UFO from yesterday was right overhead."

"You're pullin' my leg now. Red wouldn't be out in the woods on a Saturday."

"He was though. Scouting out our next job."

"You sure you didn't dream all that, Dale? You were fast asleep when I took off to hunt for more mushrooms. I been out here foraging at the rim of the clear cut this whole time, and I ain't seen Red or no flying saucer."

I glanced at the horizon. Dark thunderheads had rolled in from the Pacific just to the west and were scrambling east toward the Trinity Alps. I could smell the ocean scent being carried on the wind and mingling with the sharp aroma of redwood, cedar, and forest duff.

"We should get back to town. Storm's headed our way," I said.

"Wait till I tell Red you fell asleep on an old stump and dreamed him and that flying saucer was out here."

I hopped off the stump and followed Hank back across the clear cut and into the dense stands of timber beyond.

Come Monday, everybody on the falling crew got word that Red Black had disappeared. Had a fight with his lady friend at The Whiskey Trot on Friday night, so somebody said. The next morning she watched him drive away from the boarding house and hadn't seen him since.

A few weeks later, I broke it off with Stanette and moved to Oregon. Eventually, I lost touch with Hank and the others. But as far as I know, Red and his crummy were never found. More curious to me, I lived all over the country after that and not once did I come across another strange, luminous vessel sailing across the heavens. But I always kept my eyes peeled just in case Eureka had been something other than a wake-up call.

In Order

*"If you wish to make an apple pie from scratch,
first you must invent the universe."*
—Carl Sagan

Christine DeSimone

When I met the man whose house
would become ours, his palace of orange rinds
was shriveled into coils. Built from 1906
earthquake rubble, every board
was a moment lost. Its voice was angry:
crackling and fragile as charred powder.
It baltered like a marionette
under its shambolic order
of dust—the previous owner
had never finished painting. Or smoking.
Or tossing wine bottles behind the stove.
We scraped our brooms at chipped linoleum
and the leaves which left
their puddle-shadows on the deck.
They weren't perfect circles.
We weren't yet perfect ourselves, as if we were
testing each other to prove we were really there.

In Order

Summer took its toll as we performed
the ritual of renovation. Agitated spiders
taunted fanciful webs from the doorways.
White-fleshed silence tucked into corners.
The deck was naked, peeling, begging for bloom
We moved our bruised bones to fill big black bags
with things that no longer mattered. Does a calendar
which no longer tells time matter?
These green apples still will not bulb,
but one day we will listen to them drop in the grass
and try to guess the moment of each.
Sometimes we stand at deck's edge
and try to invent the universe.
We're broken in the same places, he declared
the first time he held my hands.
We were goddamn fools.
As if we could have anchored ourselves
to the essentials: book leaning across a gap.
Shadow of his ten-year-old cat in mid-leap.
My hand reaching out just as he was about to speak.

A.S.

James Croal Jackson

You still haunt my longing;
the lantern never was yet
burned louder some years
than others—certain days,

you were a faraway dream—
facing the tide, your black
hair and literature. The Pacific,
the Atlantic, the frozen

December we met again,
you said you were unstable—
ice drove us down dark streets,
engine idle in the middle of a lot.

It takes knowing how your face moves,
intimate and drunk in negative light,
our immovable stone eroding
in the wind of time.

Sketch of a Winnemucca Summer Night

Jeffrey Alfier

I loiter the streets alone, unremarkable—
like an actor who can only play a single role.

Between Humboldt River and the Amtrak rail,
hot winds drub the long gray street.

They fluster litter into dust devils,
smell of strangers in a bar, uneasy sleep,

lost love, diesel smoke,
and the out of place alloy of the unforeseen:

a woman's hair, still damp from the river,
a trace of salt on her skin. The kind of woman

you approach too late in the day
under the dust-tangled aura of a streetlight,

raising her palm to you, as if to signal silence,
as if to hear voices just out of reach.

No Man's Land

John P. Kristofco

The trench rose above the men, damp, cold, stinking just like them, gashed into the ground by the simple, brutish force that pushes life aside, pushes things like them aside.

The soldiers sat, stood, leaned into the turgid earth, stretched out in whatever sleep they stole in times between the shells and gas, some in contemplation of their fate; some spoke; some prayed the tattered words that held whatever faith and hope was left.

Some moaned in corners covered with blankets, green like earth veneered with frazzled grass, medics knelt beside them, exhausted with futility, the infidelity of life, knowing now more than they ever thought they'd know, begging for their lost ignorance.

Two hundred yards away, men in different uniforms leaned against the same cold earth, wrestled the same thoughts and prayers, died the same among their brothers in their ditch beneath the stars that never moved or changed.

In the space between the trenches was the land where no man walked, the contested land, the reason for the digging, the muddy measure of the weight of life.

The land was plain at dawn, brushed with fog, sun diffused across the dew like any farmer's meadow, any field. The trees that lived through shells still found their color in the light like grass, the brown stones and the gray.

But birds had gone away in the wisdom of their guileless souls. And as day rose, the field could not hide its shame, could deny its wounded truth. It was the space between the trenches where these men were summoned from their every days, their youth, to stand with no concession, no retreat, given only weapons and the idea of their uniform set against the others just like them, gathered in the dogma of the other side.

It was the space between, the killing field, the place where reason wouldn't live.

But there came a day when word went out—from whom it wasn't clear—that the business of the trenches and the space between had been decided; the war was done.

And the men stood, amazed, looking at each other in their places gouged in earth. *Could this be true?* Had the simple power of words changed their world again?

They had been so long within the earth, it was hard to rise up. But those words drew them forth, and they rose in fits and starts, a clamber here, an awkward step, a reaching hand. And as they rose above the earth and heard no sound, no shot, no volley in response, a sensation overtook their hearts and legs, and they scrambled to the light of no man's land, standing in the sun and shadows of their fear.

And as they looked across the field, they saw those on the other side, standing in the daylight just like them.

They looked across the gray-green space, straining to see, to understand. It was hard to tell; it had been a long time. They may have heard the wind, the movement in the trees, perhapsa bird, but all at once, as if there were nothing else they could do, as if they could not resist, they began to walk toward each other.

Slowly at first, as if expecting fire, mines, gas, they began to pick their way to the middle, the other side growing larger, clearer with every step. The men whispered so as to not break a spell. Soon they could hear the faint words of the others, like no sound they had ever heard before.

Two uneven, tentative lines converged like the walls of some tormented room from Poe. The uniforms were different, but they were stained with the same sweat and mud, faded and wrinkled around the same souls that now moved forward.

Both lines could see the faces of the others, and though raised in different places, lined with the sounds of different words, the eyes were the same, earnest, honest eyes, eyes that saw their own truth and purpose, eyes that missed their homes, families, eyes that felt the weight of doing what they did, of knowing they had other things to do. Eyes of guilt and pride.

And then they paused ten feet apart, each looking at the other as if looking into a dusty mirror, squinting for certainty.

The sun watched them through the clouds. The trees and grass were silent.

And then a single voice called out.

"Good morning."

A magic word again.

"Guten tag."

And the middle of that no man's land was changed as surely as if it had been touched by the hand of God.

The men stepped to each other, and the two lines became one. Some shook hands, some embraced; some just stood and smiled. Some knew the other language and spoke in halting phrases with as much meaning in their faces as in their clumsy words.

Whatever it was that brought them there, the voices that had summoned them, seemed to vanish, and the men felt the sudden flush of liberation wash over them. It was as if...

Then all at once, up the hill beyond the field, a shell exploded, and then another, and another. Below them, the men could hear the rattle of rifle rounds, machine gun fire.

It was not over. The speakers of the magic words had lied, or they had never said the words at all.

And the men in the mingled line stood back, and two rough lines re-formed. They had no rifles, knives, none of the tools of the men who brought them, those things of the trenches. They stood agape a moment, baffled now by what to do, to fight or run, to stay there out in no man's land or go back to the shadows beneath the earth.

The silent trees, the grass and rocks, the sun that arched a little further in its long, unchanging course all waited.

They paused as did the wind and dew, the cold mud of the trenches. They all paused in the silence of the land and waited for what happened next.

.

Decay

Corey S. Pressman

The sky's wide throat sings
the sweet new song:
summer's collapse
again,

told to us in bloated zucchini tongues
and by prickly-wristed pumpkin plants
    with palms open wide
        begging alms for the soil
        so it will never get old.

The dishes rest in the sink
painted thick orange by a rising light
pressed through firesky over Estacada,
east.

They will never move all day, those dishes—
    an array of perfect circles
        whose decay traces a wider circumference
        inside the house.

February, a Roadside Sumac

Nick Conrad

All winter its clustered fruit withered
and shriveled till now the sumac's branches
seem hung with trophies, so many hearts
snared and left to twist and rail before
a wind that pierces yet again. Even crows
will not dine on such fare. Later,
far off spring's green sea will drown the last
of these sad keepsakes. For now, strung up
in the freezer of a cold month,
they seem at first the remains of someone
else's disaster, these bleak valentines
that entreat obeisance from this passerby.

What Is Possible
—*Adrienne Rich*

Suzy Harris

My voice travels so far to be heard.
In this house of quiet, my voice
rattles on to the dog
who sleeps curled into herself
purring under her breath like a cat.

My voice speaks to the teakettle,
which answers with a song,
and to the refrigerator
which answers with a hum I can't hear

and through the wall
to the workers next door
laying plaster over wallboard
who walk out to the sidewalk
for a smoke and even there

What Is Possible

my voice travels, unseen,
seeking other voices. Together,
our voices travel like clouds,
cross borders easily,
falling like rain on dry lands.

Listen, a powerful voice is inside you
and outside you. Each time it rains
remember your voice in the clouds,
mine too, gathering strength.

The Rhythms of the Write
Winner, 2019 Ooligan Press Write to Publish contest in poetry

Jesse Gardner

As a child I imitated the magic of grown-ups;
apprenticing my father's jump shot,
pretending to drive my mother's Volkswagen bug.
Soon I swooned to the pen scurrying across paper
their relationship reminisces of a wand to a top hat,
when scribbles would morph to stories—I'd inhale quick.
Eyebrows lifting off like rockets when my folks wrote.
Jaw dropping like a string cut from a puppet when my folks read.
What?! Whole rooms at school, full of shelves housing spine portals?
Bet! 26 was infinity to me.
I wore my own cape in elementary grades.
A book: Digging Dudes Adventures.
A poem: Imagine That.
A rap: Pins, Needles, Rabbits and Hares
Little Jesse—with intertwined hands
swinging from Shoulder to shoulder
"Thank you. Thank you. Yes, I am a writer."

Grades, rubrics, due dates;
squinty blood shot eyes, late nights.
Tools. Word Count. Drudgery—five hundred more.

The Rhythms of the Write

Imagination in closeted memory boxes,
complete sentence answers to redundancy school of redundancy.
The last time I wrote for fun...

As an adult I imitate the magic of children.
The poem that awoke out of the window
when I gave the apple tree some speech.
The rap of my living biography over
the boom bappin' beat.
I created my own assignment—
Plug a pen underneath my ribs
Fill my courage tank to F it—
and share my energy on a mic.
Rock a 15-minute show
with words I wrote. Holy Healing.
These days I wear my arties on my arms.
A book: How to Breathe
A poem: How to Cry
A rap: How Vulnerability is a superpower
I bow down. Forehead on the ground.
Palms face up;
apprentice to the earth;
pretending to be sky.
"Thank you.
Thank you.
Yes, I'll write."

Even When We Are Not Ready

"They put their fingers into their ears because of the thunder peal, for fear of death…"

—The Holy Qur'an, 2:19

Will Donnelly

An autumn storm passed, and the sky above the sea became the inside of a pear whelk shell: a palette of soft blue and gray and pink. The beach steamed, and oats on the dunes swung heavy in the breeze, the weight of water on their stems and in their seeds.

"This is why we moved to Florida," Hamin's mother Ghaada told him when he was seventeen, standing on the shore one hot October. "We came here for this air that comes right after a rain, for this sky." But though he never said as much, Hamin knew better.

His parents brought him south when he was barely eighteen months, just weeks after he had not turned his head toward their snapping fingers, had not stopped crying at the sound of his mother's voice.

"Your son is Deaf," the pediatrician had said. "Not hard of hearing or hearing impaired. His cochlea is entirely inactive." He paused. "He will never hear at all." The doctor's face, as he said this, had been the face of someone accustomed to giving bad news. Despite the fact that Ghaada did not cry, that she looked only at her hands and then her child, that she fumbled with the pendant on her necklace, the shape of her mouth told the doctor that she wanted to speak. He handed her a box of tissues and said, "I'm sorry." Hamin, on his back, gazed at the ceiling tiles with a curious look on his toothless face, and then he smiled a toothless smile up at his mother.

A year later, Ghaada did cry, but this time they were speeding through a salt marsh at dusk, the smell of ocean in the air, coming in through the air-conditioning vents even with the windows closed. Hamin sat strapped into a car seat, from where he watched his parents speak.

"What's the matter?" Ahmed asked.

"I don't want to say," she said. "You'll think it's stupid. Or selfish."

"No I won't," he said. "I'm your husband for four years—what's wrong?"

They passed a flock of egrets taking wing, a single smooth wave gliding skyward.

"I'm crying now because of how, or why, I was so angry last year, back when the doctor first told us," she said. "I was so upset, and now I realize that it wasn't only because he was Deaf. It was for us, too, for all the work it would take, all the patience, all the sacrifices. And what a selfish thing to be thinking at a time like that!" She almost laughed.

"That's nothing to be ashamed of," Ahmed said, his hand now on her shoulder as he drove. "You were just upset because you knew you'd follow through. You knew you wouldn't give up, praise God. And look where we are now. Just look."

He pointed out the window. She watched the waves of marsh grass, the mud-caked jetties pocked with oyster shells at ebbing tide, and she took into her lungs a breath of salty air. This she would forever remember as the scent of sacrifice.

So Hamin, at twenty-one, knew better than to think that they had moved for a sky the color of a shell, or for the ocean, or even for the majesty of sunsets over water; they had moved south from Michigan for the Florida School for the Deaf and Blind. The scenery, the air, could not have mattered less. In fact, now in college and living on his own, the steam that rose off the beach after a storm was something Hamin saw only between semesters. For the remainder of the year, he lived in Arlington, Virginia.

Hamin met Miriam at Gallaudet where, in a history class in January, she translated in sign for a professor. The grace with which she moved her arms and eyes, even her feet as she stood next to the podium, had so enthralled him that he had not been able to take notes.

"You must kiss well," he signed to her over dinner a few weeks later.

"How would you know?" she asked him. "You've never kissed me."

"Kissing," Hamin signed, "is as much an act of the hands as of the lips. It involves the arms, the legs, the torso. And I have seen you speak."

"I bet, then," Miriam said, "that you are a good dancer. It involves the torso, the legs, the arms, but not so much the mouth." She smiled and tilted back her glass of wine.

"I'm a terrible dancer," Hamin said, "but I love the feel of music."

In the darkness of his bed, Miriam learned to feel Hamin's hands as he signed, and as they lay together in the night, she cupped her hands over his to feel his words.

"That we sleep together out of wedlock," she signed to him one night, "does this make you uncomfortable?"

"It makes me happy," Hamin signed back.

"Isn't it against your religion?"

"Yes," he said, "but that does not matter to me so much these days."

"Why not?"

"Islam, to me," Hamin signed, "is old men with long, white beards." He took his hands away, then placed them back in Miriam's. "In school, there was a great expanse of wood on which we prayed. It was a floor, but it felt thin and flexing beneath our knees, and in this wood, as the old men prayed or as the muezzin called, I felt the sounds there, but they meant nothing to me. They were not God. They were just vibrations in the floor. I still feel them at the mosque when I go home."

"But God does not exist only in vibration. He is everywhere." Miriam's hands moved quickly.

"You are agnostic," Hamin said. "Why does this bother you? God is also in the blasts of bombs. I cannot abide by this." Hamin breathed twice before he signed again. "Do not worry," he said. "I find truth by other means now."

"And your parents?" Miriam asked. "Do they know?"

"They don't like it, but how can I pray to a God in whom I do not believe? It would be agnostic heresy, you might say, and would be to honor a God used as a weapon." Hamin paused, holding Miriam's hands around his own. "I may go to mosque with my father, but I do not think holy thoughts while I am there."

The following October, the sun was at an autumn slant and drew long shadows in the woods. Hamin watched these shadows in the woods across the Metro tracks. The ground there was now brown, coated already with dry leaves, and the trees were nearly bare of them, skeletal, brushing stiff against the sky.

A train was coming, and Hamin stepped closer to the track, close enough so that his feet were on the warning pattern. No other passengers stood so close, and a man in a long, dark coat watched him closely and with concern. Miriam tugged at his sleeve.

"Come back," she signed to him, but he shook his head and closed his eyes.

He smelled the air, and on the breeze there was the bite of cooler nights, the dusty aroma of leaves and dry bark, much of which had already peeled from the trunks of trees and fallen to the ground. And then, as the train approached, there came a metallic scent mixed with that of engine grease and rust, and with a sudden huff, the braking train exhaled on Hamin's face, pressing his jacket up against him and his jeans against his legs. He had not seen the headlights or the angry businessman wagging a finger at him as the train pulled to a stop. He did not see anything until he felt the train braking to his left, when he stopped laughing and opened his eyes.

On board, he sat with Miriam and watched his face reflected in the glass as they climbed past Pentagon City, Reagan National, and then down through the Pentagon Station tunnel itself.

"This place has bad memories for me," Miriam signed. Hamin nodded, but his hands were folded silent in his lap.

He had been with her when, on a morning just four weeks before, he and Miriam had exited this station, back when anyone could exit the train there, before armed guards patrolled the Pentagon platform, and they had walked up the escalator and straight into a cloud of white ash. They emerged into the cloud among the coughing mass like tribal dancers, and only their eyes shone wet and darkly through the whiteness. The sun had been completely blocked. Out of the smoke came soldiers running, dressed all in black, machine guns strapped across their shoulders. They ran out of the cloud, then faded into it again, barking directions, their mouths open as in chorus but with ash-burned eyes and tears running down their faces, washing tracks across their faces through the cinder. They were ghosts or demons, things born of nightmare landscapes, and in their movements lived a kind of chaos, the likes of which Hamin had never seen.

For Hamin, as always, the scene had been silent, but he had felt the noises clanging in his bones, blaring, picking at vibratoed air, at the hair on the back of his neck and on his arms. He had never heard a sound, yet in his sleeping dreams of the event, he could hear, or at least he dreamed he could. It was a smearing sound, difficult to parse from the disarray, but he knew that what he heard had been the sound of people screaming.

"This is not Islam," his father typed into the TDD receiver on the night of the event. "The people who did this were murderers. They were not true Muslims."

"I know," Hamin typed, after a pause.

"It's people like this who will be the death of our culture, who will destroy it. How will we ever recover from this?"

Hamin typed nothing.

"Your mother has worried about you today. Please tell her you're okay."

"Mom, I'm okay," Hamin typed.

"Have you been going to mosque?" his father asked.

"Yes," Hamin replied, but this was a lie.

Hamin and Miriam met Miriam's sister, Angela, at Rosario's for dinner, where they shared a crystal pitcher of sangria on the patio.

"I'm a little embarrassed to ask," said Angela, "but do you read lips?"

"Yes," Hamin said. "But not so well from a distance."

"Can you read *my* lips?" she said, mouthing the words but not using any sound.

"I can tell you're not speaking," said Hamin. "Your mouth moves differently when you're not actually talking."

Angela laughed.

At a table behind Hamin, a pair of couples, two men and two women, were eating dinner. "I don't get," one woman said, "how a religion of so-called peace can cause all that destruction. It's insane. What sort of prophet tells people to kill people?"

One of the men broke in. "Look, you're blaming the entire Muslim world for the actions of a few crazies—"

"Who justified their actions with their *religion*," the woman said. "You can't get around that. I don't know how they feel about this war, but those people are asking for it."

Angela shot Miriam a worried glance.

"What?" said Miriam. "He agrees with them, you know." She motioned to Hamin.

"With whom?" said Hamin.

"There's a woman at the table behind you saying that Islam is causing all the problems, all the violence."

"Yes, I agree," said Hamin.

Miriam sighed.

"I'm an atheist," Hamin said. "Islam is not a race." He slid his chair back and stood, folding his napkin on the table. "Excuse me," he said aloud to the table behind him. "Excuse me, but which one of you was talking about Islam?"

The couples grew silent, their faces flushing pink. Sheepishly, the woman who'd been speaking raised her hand. "It was me," she said. "I'm sorry, I'm really sorry—"

"No, I agree with you. I do, one hundred percent. The world would be a better place without any sort of organized religion."

"See?" the woman said. "Exactly. He knows it too. Thank you."

Hamin returned to his chair.

Darkness had arrived, and above the street, bats swung in low arcs beneath the vapor lamps. To the east, a Chinook helicopter rose into the sky and chopped the air.

A server brought steaming plates of pollo asado and a cold bucket of ceviche and set them on the table. "Is there anything else I can get you?" he asked, but there were only silence and the sounds of cutting knives.

"How could you possibly feel that way?" Miriam asked him later that night, as they lay together in darkness, her hands against his so he could feel her words. "I'm not Muslim, and even I know that those people were out of their minds. How could you think those people represent your culture?" Her hands moved quick and hard and rough.

"They may be misinterpreting things," Hamin said to her. "But they are of my culture, my beliefs. It makes me doubt my past sometimes. As I said before, what kind of God promotes such violence?"

"But that's just it, Hamin—no God promotes this! They are absolutely wrong! And evil!" Hamin could feel her sigh before she placed her hands back in his.

"I don't know," Hamin said. "I don't know."

Miriam rolled over and pulled the sheet on top of her, and Hamin could feel her every movement. He felt her arm twitch, her breath, the blinking of her eyes. He watched the window form a prism as a car passed on the street outside, and, some time later in the night, his mind drifted away into blackness.

The late November night when Ghaada called her son, the first flurries of snow already stirred the air in Washington. They spun as much up as down and seemed not to fall but simply to materialize, piling in little heaps along tree branches and blades of brown grass, whipping through the city. Hamin was watching the spinning flurries through the window from the darkness of his desk when the telephone light began to flash.

"Hello?" he typed.

"Hamin, this is your Mama. You must come home," was the reply. "A terrible thing has happened."

Many windows had been broken in their house. Hamin looked toward the beach through the glass edges, sharp as razors, and he felt the ocean wind against his face. The carpet in the living and dining rooms sopped with water, but had now dried to a gentle dampness. There was a smell of mold.

"We were out to dinner, praise God," Ahmed said to Hamin. "But they took everything. Look at this place. They even took your baseball cards. And they left it just like this."

Ghaada stayed at the hotel. She could not bear to see her home destroyed, paint sprayed all over the walls and so much missing. A home, Hamin thought, can become a memory manifest: with it comes some good, some bad, and it can never fully let us go. There was pain in each broken mirror, in the rags stuffed into drains so that they flooded, spilling water onto floors, but the worst was the graffiti on the walls.

IRAQI GO HOME, it said, and in another place, across an ancient hanging rug, a gift from Hamin's deceased grandfather: WE WILL BURY YOU ALIVE.

"Do you know who did it?" Hamin asked.

"No, but the police, they are working on it. For now, we can't stay here. It will be weeks before we can get this place ready to move back in, and your mother and I, to be honest, Hamin, we don't know if we want to live here anymore."

At mosque on Saturday, Hamin and his father bowed their heads. Hamin watched the cleric's lips as he mouthed the words, and he tried to think of school, but his memories interrupted him.

The cleric was a young man, probably no more than thirty, and as he spoke he held a string of prayer beads in his hands. All this seemed far away to Hamin, as though his childhood were being exhumed.

When Hamin was young, he had watched the older cleric's beard move softly as he spoke and his mouth moving inside it. The older cleric's voice had been as clear as a tuning fork as it reverberated through the wood. Hamin could feel it in his knees. The younger cleric was not so loud, or perhaps his voice was higher. The vibrations of the voice were softer. His was a peaceful voice, and Hamin meditated on the peace within it.

For his eighteenth birthday, his parents had given Hamin a special alarm clock with a flashing light.

"It has five alarm settings," his father said, his eyes smiling. "This is your very own muezzin call. It will tell you when to pray."

"Thank you," Hamin had said, then stuffed it in his suitcase, and it now sat on the top shelf of his apartment closet. He had already taken the batteries out and used them in a flashlight. But in Florida, he did not need the clock. His father told him when it was time to pray, even waking him at dawn, tapping him on the shoulder and guiding him to the prayer rugs. Above them, he had made a niche in the hotel room ceiling, pointing toward the East.

"It's small," Ahmed said. "No one will ever notice it."

Ahmed prayed, but Hamin only knelt and did not bow. He thought of Miriam instead.

"Why don't you bow?" Ahmed asked. "It is time to pray."

Hamin did not know what to say.

"Prayer," his father said, "is an act of love. It is something that we do even when we are not ready. And it is an action, a movement of the body forward. God is a physical being as well as a spiritual one."

"What would you say," Hamin asked, "if I did not believe in Him? I'm not saying that, but if I did."

"I would say it was your choice," his father said.

Hamin stood up and sat on the bed. His father watched him for a moment, then bowed and mumbled prayers toward the East.

When Hamin and Ahmed went to the house again, they set up rented drying fans and sprayed the walls with paint remover. They wore gloves and scrubbed at the paint, Ahmed brushing with long sweeping motions and Hamin moving quickly in short, scrubbing movements, wanting all of this to be done. As the autumn sun rose, the house grew warmer.

"No power," his father signed. "No air conditioning."

Hamin wiped the sweat from his eyes and continued scrubbing, but when he stood back, he saw that the marks of his brush only formed the dirty shapes of the words that had been painted there. The entire wall would have to be repainted.

In the dining room, a can of paint had been thrown. Red liquid dripped onto the carpet and flowed in little runnels down the wall like spattered blood. It had ruined a credenza as well, coating the top in a thick red shell, and Hamin saw that he would have to move the credenza to clean the wall behind it.

It was heavy, but he lifted one end and then the other, noticing the feet of the object where they had made indentations in the carpet, and next to one of the indentations, he found a champagne cork. This, the remnant of some celebration, may have popped from out the neck of a champagne bottle many years ago. It was dry in his hand, and he turned it to see if it was labeled, but it was not. The champagne, of course, would have been non-alcoholic, but Hamin enjoyed the thought of his parents hosting a party, surprising guests with champagne, and then losing the cork.

Next to where the cork had been, Hamin found a photograph. Curled and yellowing with age, a corner had been marred with paint, but still the image was clear. It was his father many years before, thinner, with more hair, and standing next to him, Hamin. They were on a bright summer beach, the wind tossing their hair, his father holding Hamin's hand. With their free hands they were making the sign that meant "how are you?" toward the camera. On the back of the photograph, Hamin read in his mother's cursive writing: "first sign."

Perhaps it had been on display. Perhaps the flying cork had knocked it down.

"Where did you find this?" his father said, tapping Hamin on the shoulder.

"On the floor, by the wall."

His father smiled. "So many things we learned together, you and I," he said. "We wouldn't be here at all if it had not been for you.

Look at this photograph. Close your eyes and feel the photo's creases, feel all the hands that have passed across its edges. This I used to carry with me in my pocket. It is many years old now."

Hamin closed his eyes and felt the folds of the photo paper, the softness of its edges, the creases that matched the creases in the palms of his own hands. He imagined the years that it had spent inside his father's pocket, there with keys and coins, folded by his father's hand and placed, perhaps, at night upon his dressing table. Hamin traced the creases with his fingers and, in silence, smelled the paint that now stiffened it in places, and he imagined Miriam, her hands around his in the darkness of his bed. He thought of how she spoke to him through touch, how much her hands had said to him at night, and how the photo, like her hands, contained the vestiges of movement, the history of a life within its lines.

When he opened his eyes, his father said to him, "Put it in your pocket now. Take it home with you," and then his father turned and walked into the living room.

Hamin followed him. The sun had risen high enough that it shone only overhead, and they could no longer see it over the ocean.

The prayer rugs were wet. Hamin knelt down beside his father, and water squeezed out of the fibers and into his jeans. They would have to move the rugs away from the broken windows by the afternoon, by the time it rained. Already, clouds were knitting in the sky; already, he could smell the coming storm.

"They ruined this house," Ahmed said, "and yet they didn't touch the arrow towards Mecca." He pointed upward to where, on the ceiling, there was a small triangle pointing to the east-southeast. "And they helped us find a photograph. Allahu Akbar," he said.

Hamin looked out to sea. The waves there moved and curled like flexing sheets of glass.

"Allahu Akbar," Hamin said.

Ahmed lowered his body, and Hamin, the ocean breeze cool against his face, formed with his hands the prayer to Mecca and with his mouth the words. He bowed until his forehead touched the floor.

San Simeon

Chad Bartlett

Small children cry and pull at shirts, more interested in a hotel pool they've been promised than the colonnade's blue-white echo. A walk-in fireplace provides little joy after hours on the highway. Nothing impresses them. They have, after all, seen it all before, arrogance and awe, desperate scratchings along tall, white walls, palm trees towering over cities, larger than death. Fear is like this, big and gilded, threatening in concentric circles outward from the one who owns it, a child's hard candy dropped into water, implausibly blue.

Breaking with Still Life at the Ranch Motel, Opelousas, Louisiana

Jeffrey Alfier

3:20 a.m., and the widening horn of Acadiana Rail
seeped through my window, softly breaking my sleep
like the touch of a night nurse.

From my bed, I lean toward the window,
listened to the sound drift to silence, the way
late-comers finally did, a few doors down.

Between two notes of the horn's retreat,
the hard slam of a door. Someone startled
out of sleep, realizing they never went home.

Their footfalls hurried over pavement,
as another in the room they shared
rolled over, only to wake to the next train,

8:10 a.m.—an alarm they did not set,
how they'd slumbered so deeply
as to nearly miss that sudden sound.

The Dark Inside

Chelsea Thiel

Inside the bunker the man made
a marionette of his wife
by tethering strings to her hands
and feet to make her dance,
and one through her chin
to make her speak and sing.
He runs a bow across the exposed
cords of her neck eliciting his lament.

It looks an awful lot like love and the devil
is a handsome man. His horns are ornate, her smile
embroidered. He stands on stilts
to puncture the sky with needles, stitching dawn
to dusk, removing
the day, so that he may spend every night—
only night—loving his wife to pieces.

The Card-Counter

Jeffrey S. Chapman

There are some days when it is okay to call in sick, or even just be late. I'm 30 weeks pregnant and my divorce was finalized this afternoon. *This* afternoon. My boss would understand. But I've never missed work or been late and I won't start today. I am more presentable at 30 weeks than most of the dealers are on their best days. My ridiculous, rainbow-colored vest is spotless, my shirt and slacks are pressed. I will not let the dust and the desert defeat me.

The casino floor is busy until around two or three in the morning, when the drunk party people go to their rooms. Now there's just a scattering of sad souls and a handful still getting lucky.

Each blackjack table has only one or two players. We dealers shift to a new table every half hour and end up back at each table every two hours. We get a half-hour break every four hours, which is good because standing for so long kills my back and my feet. My pit boss tells me I can sit on a stool, but I don't think that's professional.

By the time I return to any given table there are usually new players. People lose their money or move on before two hours are up. Tonight there is one kid who has been at the same table all night. He was there at 10 o'clock, midnight, 2 o'clock, and now 4 o'clock. He is not doing well. He has not been doing well all evening. His stack has been short all night. Early on he was playing with friends, but I haven't seen them in a long time.

When I come back to the table at 2:30, I ask him where his friends are.

"They drove home," he says. "It's an hour and a half drive. Some of them have work tomorrow."

"Why didn't you go with them?" I ask.

"I'm down. I have to win it back," he says.

"Good luck," I say.

He gives me a small, obligatory smile.

He must be around 25. He looks clean and mild. He doesn't talk to other players; he just concentrates on his cards and watches as I deal to the other players. When I finish that shift, he has lost almost all the chips in front of him.

At 4:30, he's still there. He's drooping a little, tired. His luck hasn't changed.

"How much have you lost, honey?" I ask.

"Nine hundred dollars," he says.

"Is that a lot for you?" I ask.

He nods, stone-eyed.

"I should be winning. I'm counting cards."

"You shouldn't tell me that."

For some people, $900 would be chump change, a single bet, and for other people, it will derail their entire year and get them into real trouble. It's our job not to care. You might be losing your child's college fund and I'll deal you another hand. But I feel for this kid.

I know the sex of my baby. It's a boy. I have two other kids but they're both girls. I don't really know how it will work now that I'll be a single mother of three in a town far away from my family. I'd move back home, but I can't take the kids from their dad. That wouldn't be fair. He isn't a bad man, or a bad dad. But it's hard being young and married in a small town because you are around each other every minute of every day. We just realized that we don't like each other that much. And I realize I shouldn't have followed him here, but I did.

"Why are you still here, honey?" I ask the boy. "Why don't you just cut your losses?"

He tilts his head one way, then the other, thinking about it.

"I have to get it back. I have to wait for my luck to turn."

"It might not turn."

"A girl broke up with me two days ago. She just stopped talking to me. Everything was going great and then suddenly she broke up with me."

"I'm sorry," I say.

"I really liked her."

I understand that moment. He will know more pain later on in life, but it probably doesn't feel like that to him right now.

He puts his hands flat on the table in front of him.

"I need my luck to turn," he repeats.

I agree.

He's watching the cards I'm dealing. He's keeping track of the deck. A series of 4s and 5s and 6s come out. I know, as does he, that this makes that deck favorable. There's a much better chance of blackjack now, and of the dealer busting.

He looks me straight in the eyes and moves his entire stack of chips, around $100, out into his circle. Again, for many players, that's not a big bet, but for this kid it is. It will put him down $1000 for the night. It means he knows he has very good odds.

I should tell my pit boss that he's counting, but it's small stakes, and I want him to win.

The Card-Counter

He gets a ten, I get a five, he gets a king and holds. My hidden card is a four and I deal a queen, so he wins.

He lets it all ride.

He gets another twenty. Good. I start out with a two, which is great for him. My second card is a king. Also very good for him. But then I deal a nine. Twenty-one. He loses it all. There was about a 10% of that card hitting. It's how his luck has gone all night, I know. He doesn't even react. He leaves his drink and his coat at the table and walks over to the nearest ATM. He comes back with a stack of one hundred dollar bills. Ten of them. He places them in front of me to change for chips.

I am not supposed to discourage him. I have a job to do. I am professional. The casino is built around taking money from people like him. Almost every person in here has a similar sad story and they have made their own choices. But I know this kid isn't playing for the money, he's playing for a woman.

"Is that your rent money?" I ask.

"The next two months."

I cover his money with my hand. One thousand dollars. This shift is going to be over in 20 minutes. A couple drunks are cheering at the one remaining craps table. At least they are having good luck. The lights blink. The bells ring. Slot machines jangle.

I want to tell him to take his money back. I want to refuse to take it. I want to call the pit boss over and tell him the kid is cheating so that he will throw him out and save him from himself. I want to tell him that she won't love him, even if he wins. I want to tell him that love isn't made to last. I want him to be safe, forever. I want this baby to be safe, forever.

But. I smile at him and start counting out stacks of red chips, green chips, black chips. I am a professional.

"Let's go," I say. "Let's turn your luck around."

Perpetual Summer

Linda Neal

I want this season, fall, to fall all over me.
I yearn for the singular beating of autumnal drums,
for caterwauling foghorns and a season of hail.

I want it to start in September. I want it to sound
like trombones, last until pelicans breed
and grey waves pound against the seawall.

The bulbs I planted lie just under the surface
of dead space between summer and a brick heat
spreading long hot days that should be autumn.

The air doesn't know rain. Last week, I lay under my ceiling fan
waiting for night to fall, waiting for magnolia leaves to fall,
waiting to welcome the wild destiny of thunder clouds
to cover the corner of the garden, waiting for seasons to die

into each other, the way they used to when rainstorms came
from the north, loud as a locomotive
and our wind-whipped collars beat against our cheeks,

Perpetual Summer

my boys and me, running into the library or the laundromat
or racing to the car with bags of groceries, as the storm blew
a chill against our cheeks and lips.

We rubbed our hands against each other's
and the wild beach air flew up the narrow streets.
I want the wind and the chill back, a discrete season,
not these hot and hotter days and weeks and months
that fuse the seasons into blue.

I want my boys back, not these men who live in houses of their own.
I want the wild air that whipped rain and sand around us,
that bared us to the elements and each other.

The Cure for Acne

Mark Rubin

When a dad relies on Christ
for backup, as in *Christ, what do you mean
she's kind of pregnant*, what follows
can't be good. For Ben it means

the cure for acne is sex,
his seed compounding in layaway
like money in a secret account.
He's done the math. He can't afford to give

a rat's ass for Pythagoras or crybaby *c*
waiting by a bus stop for the square root
of *a*-squared + *b*-squared, who heard *humming
of strings, music in the spacing of spheres.*

Under his blank face his yearbook reads
Most Likely to Disappear—a foreshadowing
of life in low relief, a shape in sawdust
carved from his family tree. In fifty years,

The Cure for Acne

Ben-time, back bent like an obtuse angle
("Isn't that you-know-who, what's his name?"),
he'll be known for his civic solution
to public urination—a urinal made from

a Styrofoam cup and hose long enough
to reach the street, sitting proof,
Necessity is the mother of invention.
Plato aside, for now for Ben it means

he's thrown his last fastball into a pitch-back
net rusting in the yard, the last he'll pretend
to hear, each time the ball returns,
Good pitch, son.

The Hiding Place

Evan Morgan Williams

The man and his wife left the motel early to visit a few of the old sights—the bridge, the bonsai garden, the bell tower—but they cut short the tour and met their daughter at her apartment around noon. It was an old brick walk-up called the Rosemont, and it was the only four-story building on University Drive, but neither the man nor his wife could recall it from their college days and, anyway, they did not agree on anything anymore.

Most of their daughter's things were boxed and waiting by the curb. A few parents were helping their kids lug boxes and furniture, but graduation had been a week ago, and most of the rooms were cleared out. The daughter's room, on the fourth floor, was a climb. Her window looked over the lawn and trees. The man could see the bell tower of the university chapel through the trees, although soon the trees would be too leafy for that.

Gazing down at the lawn, the man spotted a purple fairy ring in the grass, and this spurred a memory. He turned from the window. His daughter's room was small, a studio. The girl stood at the bed, folding shirts and sweaters and packing them in a box. The man walked over and stood next to her, and, very deliberately, set his hands on the bed's carved footboard. It was exactly right. The bed was mounted on a track, allowing it to slide into a recess in the wall, appearing like a built-in cabinet when not in use. His daughter's books were on the shelf above the headboard, a few novels and poetry books he knew she would never read again. The man remembered the unusual bed, and he remembered the fairy rings in the grass, and he remembered being in the Rosemont before. Back when he was in school, he had spent a night in one of these rooms, on one of these beds, on a girl's yellow sheet, his arms around the girl. He pulled back his hands from his daughter's bed.

"I don't fucking believe it."

"Dad!"

"Sorry. I forgot something, that's all. I mean I remembered something."

"Mom can get it. She's down at the car." The girl set down a folded pink sweater she had worn a few times but didn't wear anymore. She went over to the window and started to lean out. "What was it?"

"No, no, it's nothing like that. It's not a thing. It's not an item. It's just that I remember being here before, that's all. Listen, I'll be right back."

The girl resumed packing clothes into the box. She was humming a tune the man did not recognize. "Don't be gone long," she said. "There's a lot of boxes still."

The man went down the stairs. Solid mahogany banister. Newell post. Marble steps. Back in the day, the Rosemont must have been something special. Coved ceilings, leaded glass windows, wrought iron fixtures, mahogany trim. Now the wind blew through the rooms and slammed the doors. The trees along the street were shedding their caftans, and the caftans blew in and snagged on the wrought iron. At the third-floor landing, the chandelier was gone.

On the last set of stairs, the man passed two older men: the apartment manager and a priest, maybe from the local parish. They were going room to room, loading bags with college sweatshirts and books and cookware, anything good the students had left. Maybe it was for a thrift store. The priest's shoes clicked on the marble steps.

The man's wife stopped him in the foyer. She was carrying up a bucket of sponges and cleaners. Her face looked tired. They had argued on the drive from the motel. He couldn't remember why. He never remembered why.

She said, "We have to leave it spotless to get the deposit back."

He said, "Most of these kids just leave everything, their whole lives, left behind."

"Where are you going?"

"I forgot something."

"What?"

"Um, a letter."

"A letter? You wrote a letter? Can't you just tell her? Why do you have to make it a fucking letter?"

"It's hard to explain. Hey, guess what. I think I remember this place."

"No you don't."

"Remember Sarah O'Brien?"

"Yeah. What about her?"

"She and I fucked in here. No, we made love."

"Fuck you, honey."

"I love you too. See you upstairs."

He went outside and around to the lawn. He passed the dumpster filled with books, clothes, crumpled posters, cases of empty bottles, dented lamp shades. Someone had heaved a stained mattress against the side of the dumpster. As the man walked across the lawn, his legs parting the tall grass, everything became familiar and focused. *Watch out for the fairy rings,* Sarah O'Brien had said, taking his hand and tugging him on a crooked path through the grass. The man came to the utility stairs in back. The door to the stairs was unlocked. He stepped around empty bottles and a water dish the students had put out for strays. The stairs were steep and creaky and dark and narrow, and he climbed three flights because he remembered three. He would know the exact door by a key hidden on a nail above the trim. Sarah O'Brien had called it the secret key, and there it was. He knocked on the door, just to be sure. Nothing. Good. He turned the key, opened the door, and tiptoed into the kitchen.

What had happened to her? Where had she gone? Was it Santa Cruz? Why did she have to meet that guy? That fucker. The apartment was quiet. He slid across the linoleum where they had sat and smoked weed and waited for Pop-Tarts to bake.

He glided onto the parquet floor of the first room and ducked beneath the chandelier. Boxes from a liquor store lay along the windows, partly filled with books. Dresses hung from a hook on the closet door. The front door was shut, and the latch was rattling in the breeze. A guitar in an open case lay on the floor. He slid to the bedroom. He could see the bed rolled out from the wall. He could see the ornate footboard. Exactly the same. He stopped.

A boy and girl lay asleep in the sunshine. Sheet pulled up. The girl's long black hair was tangled down her cheek. The sheet was draped over their bodies, and their bodies were knotted together. The man inched forward. He put his hand on the footboard and gripped it, the patterns carved into the wood. He knew the patterns. He watched the sheet rise and fall.

He tiptoed out of the room.

The Hiding Place

Halfway down the back stairs, he met the manager coming up, and he paused on the narrow landing to let the manager pass.

"You're Alice's father, yes?" The manager was carrying a bag and stuffing it with empty beer bottles. "A nice girl, she is. None of this junk. None of those boys tom-catting around. A nice good Catholic girl."

"She does have a boyfriend. In fact, she—"

"These are the wrong stairs, by the way. She's on the other side"

"I know."

"So what are you doing up here?"

"My wife and I went to the U in the eighties. I was just—"

The manager peered at him in the dark stairwell. "Did you live here once? I don't recognize you, and I've been here twenty-five years."

"Oh, I've been in here before. Say, what's that you had out there?" He wanted to change the subject.

"I found a chandelier out in the grass. It's a shame. Who would do such a thing?"

"Well, I'll see you." The man continued down the narrow stairs.

"Wait. What did you say you were you doing up here?"

"I forgot something, that's all." His hands felt empty, and he gripped the steep banister, not for balance but to have something to hold.

He went around to the front of the building, climbed the marble stairs to the fourth floor, and opened the door of his daughter's room. She was still working by the bed, but now she was packing sheets and blankets. She put a pink blanket in a box. The man remembered when his wife had put that same blanket on her own dorm bed, and he had slept on it many times.

The Hiding Place

"Dad, what's wrong?"

"Nothing. But hey, check this out. There's a secret hiding place."

"What?"

"Look." He kneeled at the foot of the bed, the ornate carvings beneath his fingertips, and he pried a false panel off the footboard. The fit was tight, and the varnish on the mahogany cracked loudly, but the panel popped off. The little hiding place was empty.

"Oh my god, cool. How did you know about this?" She bent down next to him, her face very close to his, and she was smiling wonderfully like a little girl. Then she frowned.

His wife came out of the kitchen. She said, "Alice, make sure you label what goes with us, what goes with you." She went back into the kitchen. She was running water into her bucket.

The man replaced the panel on the footboard. It was tight. He fit it in as good as he could get it, but it wasn't perfect anymore.

"You can sell most of my stuff, Dad."

"The CDs?"

"Some of the CDs."

"The pretty dresses."

"The dresses, Dad." She smiled.

The girl put on a hooded sweatshirt with the university colors and 05 on the back. She reached back and pulled her braid out of the collar. Her long wavy hair, which he had always liked, was tight and pulled back now. Later in the day, his wife was taking her to a salon. Probably get one of those smooth cuts that tapered at the neck, the same as every girl. Every woman.

She was packing a dust buster. That would be good to have.

"Do you need anything?" He always asked that.

"No, Dad." She was taping the box shut.

"Are you happy?" He asked that too, and she always said yes, but he asked anyway because he wanted her to be happy even though he couldn't do anything about it.

She set down the box and looked at him. "Are you happy, Daddy?"

"Sure," he said. Damn happy. He'd better be happy. After everything that might have gone wrong in twenty-five years, he was damn happy. He thought about the night long ago in that girl's room. They were happy. Her name was in his mouth. Sarah. They were so happy they wrote it all down on a sheet of paper and hid it away in the hiding place. Was Sarah happy now? He was happy. Everybody was happy. He was forty-six years old, and he was fucking happy. He had worked this fucking hard, he'd better be fucking happy, and he'd paid a hundred thousand to this fucking Catholic university just so his daughter could decide to…be happy. It wasn't what he'd expected, but it should have been, and he could not get over that. To take away all of her pain was supposed to be his job. That mattered even more than being happy. It wasn't supposed to be that way, but that's the way it was. Let me take your pain.

"I don't have any pain, Daddy."

"I didn't say anything."

"Yes, you did."

His arm was around her shoulder, pulling her close the way he did when she was a little girl and she would cry and turn her face so he couldn't see. But she wasn't crying today. He was the one who wanted to cry.

The wife came back from the kitchen. "Did you ever find your damn letter?"

"Letter?" The girl had squirmed out of his arms, and she was placing a framed picture of her boyfriend in a small box with other pictures and letters, which she lifted carefully to her chest. She was looking at her mom and dad, and she looked a little scared.

"I couldn't find it." He looked at the footboard.

"Well, here's some paper then." His wife held out a pad of blank paper ready for new words.

Unsavory

Chelsea Thiel

Spare me your insipid flavor
dried and preserved into
jars above the stovetop

stored on the edge of an overstuffed shelf
in the confines of your kitchen

i attempt to preserve

stirring the pot
knocking salt onto linoleum
spilling hostile flakes of red

pouring honey
raw and distilled
into milk

to dilute
you

the recipe remains
inedible

A House for Tiny Spirits

Holly Day

When I die, trap my soul in a birdcage
With a little plastic bath, and a plastic bowl for food
Wrap the bars in cellophane so I can't slip through

Because I will never be ready to go.

I will learn all the right songs to convince your guests
That it's a bird in the cage, and not your dead wife—
I will finally learn how to whistle in key.

You're Not Wrong Forever

Ben Slotky

My four year old is screaming, howling. I can hear him, I jerk out of bed, and I come running. His room is close to mine, close to ours, so it doesn't take long, not at all, it never does. I am there in an instant, in a flash, but in that instant? In that instant, this is what it is.

It is all heat and night and running.

It is a child screaming, scared.

It is Daddy Daddy Come Here.

It is panic, it is sinking, it is what is happening, it is what do I do.

It is, is it too late.

It is this, a sinking panic, again and again, two or three or five times a week. Daddy, he says again, and I am coming, I am running, clamoring and shambling. I trip on nothing because I know where everything is. I see his door, it is right there, like always, like last night or maybe two nights ago. A knob to turn, and then the door will open and I do not know what to do, what I will do when I get there, but I know that I will do something, because I always do.

A scream and a scream.

Daddy, and I open his door and see his tear-streaked face in the weak light from the Spider Man night-light, the light that seemed bright enough before, brighter than the other night-lights. This is the one, Daddy, but isn't now or anymore. He is standing on the bed, it is night, and he is scared, screaming.

They are coming to get me, he says, Panting.

They are coming to get me. And I look at him. And he looks at me. Eyes wide, full of tears. Face red and streaked and breathing and breathing. And he is looking around and he is scared, at night in his room, again, and like before.

They are coming to get me, he says, and I say then you better shut up.

He stops.

I say this quietly. A whisper, a hush and a shush. I say this again. I lean in, conspiratorially. This is between me and him.

I say if they're coming to *get* you?

I say it like that. I lean in closer.

Then you better be quiet, or they're going to *hear* you.

I look at him. A quick nod, an eyebrow raised, and we are quiet now.

It is quiet now.

This is new, I think, and I think why I haven't thought of this before, this tactic, this plan. This seems to makes sense. This came out of nowhere, it came and got me, this idea did. He is confused by this.

I am confused by this. This makes so much sense. We are stunned by all the sense this makes, he and I are. We stand there, looking at each other, understanding flowing back and forth and back and forth. Something passed along, something imparted. They are gone now, we both know this, we can see this now, now in the Spider Man light, so I put him back in bed, kiss his sweet head, and walk, calmly and quietly out of the room.

My wife says she doesn't think that was funny, not even a little bit, even though it is, and she knows it is. She is smiling and trying not to. She tells me this in the morning. My son and I are eating breakfast together, rested and refreshed. We look at each other over our eggs. We smile. My wife tries to frown. That's not funny at all, she says again. She is wrong, but that is OK, because I am wrong sometimes, too. It is OK to be wrong, I tell her, because even if you're wrong, you're not wrong forever. This sounds like advice, I think. Like something people would say, something people smarter than I am would say and maybe have said for a long time. I wonder where it came from. I think about saying it sometime, maybe to my son, if they haven't gotten him yet.

Learning to Hear Again*

Suzy Harris

The snow falls straight and true
covering yards and sidewalks,
while I shelter under a sturdy roof,
warmed by tea and the steady heat of a gas fireplace.

All this, and quiet too,
quiet enough to read aloud
and hear the words echo in my head,
roll around so I can taste their salty-sweetness.

For so many years, I have lost
beginnings and endings, vowels and consonants,
studying faces and gestures
to confirm or deny what might have been said.

In three days, I will be like an infant again,
awash in new sounds, like a toddler
pointing *what's this?* and *what's this?*
wanting and needing to know the world,

each sticky, wondrous bit,
each chime and bell and faint clank,
each creaky floorboard,
each soft voice and spoken word.

Tell me, what is the sound of snow falling?
What is the sound branches make
as they bend under the weight of snow?
And do camellias sigh when snow
      covers their scarlet blooms?

Be patient with me. I'm learning.

On anticipating activation of my cochlear implant

Just Like This

John Sibley Williams

Empty worktable. Shavings unblown from the unfinished object. Then dust. One night, then another. Only the idea remains; if it matters anymore, a birdhouse, I think. This

ecosystem of knife & whittle, vision & hand, floodlit in a basement no one remembers how to enter. Hairspace cracks widen incrementally each year until the earth with all

its living swallows the foundations. Like taillights rounding a curve on a midnight road, the heating lamps sputter & go out. The silence comes to a delicate boil, spills over.

The dead shiver. The birds he pictured gorging on its narrow oak ledge have been replaced twice over. Their children still hungry, making due with hunger. Awl in my pocket. Dulled. Shame.

Cassandra in Three Acts

Tim Gillespie

Act I: The Trophy
Haughty in his narrow victory at Troy,
the mighty King of Argos, Agamemnon,
(genius general of the hollow wooden horse,
whose jeweled, gold-pocked façade concealed
the violence huddled inside, waiting in the dark),
took when he won what he thought he deserved.
"You can do anything," he said, "when you're a star."
Part of his loot-grab was Cassandra, the dark-skinned
royal daughter of the slaughtered Trojan tribe,
his trophy concubine. Old Agamemnon wanted
her to prove his might, and also craved
to have her use her gift to see his fate.

Act II: Her Gift
Cassandra was the same girl chased in earlier years
and twice-cursed by Apollo. Drawn by her light,
the Sun God too had moved on her—you can do
anything when you're a star—and lured her
with a shiny bauble. That glittery gift: to see the future.
Attracted by the trinket, she'd given up a covert kiss,
but when Apollo pressed for more, she pushed him off.

Rebuffed, the Sun God thrust on her a second gift
that cursed the first: thenceforth, whatever fate
the girl foresaw would never be believed. And so
down through the tidal shifts of time, Cassandra lives on,
the one who tries to sing of danger, who warns of what
we can't or won't foresee, who drowns in desperate knowledge
of the seas of sorrow still to come but clings to hope
her song will find a shore, though no one listens.

Act III: Cassandra Redux
Tonight my granddaughter is Cassandra
in the production at her high school of the *Oresteia*,
Aeschylus' ancient recounting of this timeworn tale.
She plays the role committed to that desperate,
urgent Trojan girl. At 16, Shawnie understands
Cassandra's madness, the hurt of being unheard,
the cruelty and attraction of Apollo's cocksure charm,
the devastation of a tribe's diminishment. She gets
the sting at being dismissed for being a girl; for being
too young, too smart; for having darker skin; for holding
fiercely to her trust that there are truths that can be known.
When preening men of power who think they're stars or suns
offer you a curse they claim is a gift, she knows: resist.

They can't just do anything. Let them be forewarned
that here's a girl who won't be grabbed except by truths
she won't stop telling, that here's a girl who won't
be lured by hollow jeweled things, that this girl's
no one's trophy, this girl's fate is not to go unheard.
No, Shawn, we need to hear. We might
believe you this time. Sing it.

Advice from the Oregon Iris

Madronna Holden

Don't blame the sirens
who happened to be
singing to their Mother Ocean
when your boat came along.

What you took for wreckage
was only beauty holding its own
like the Oregon iris
named tenax/*tenacity*—
since ropes braided from it
could not be broken

(These were ropes that
kept their promises).

True, their bloom
might crash the eyes
of passers-by with their
delicate surprises.

Advice from the Oregon Iris

True, they might turn
forest shadows purple
as accused

And their tongues spark
with tiny white stars eager
to tell you everything.

But you can't blame the iris
for your own flowered tongue.

Your song heard
by the sea whether
or not passers-by
tie themselves up
against hearing it.

Your own story
longing to proclaim itself
through blooming.

Contributors

Jeffrey Alfier's recent books include *Fugue for a Desert Mountain, Anthem for Pacific Avenue,* and *The Red Stag at Carrbridge: Scotland Poems*. His publication credits include *Poetry Ireland Review, The Carolina Quarterly,* and *Midwest Quarterly*.

Diane Averill's first book, *Branches Doubled Over With Fruit,* (University of Florida Press) was a finalist for the 1991 Oregon Book Award as was her second book, *Beautiful Obstacles,* in 1998. (Blue Light Press.) Her work appears in many literary magazines and anthologies. Diane is a graduate of the M.F.A. program at the University of Oregon, where she won the annual award for the best poem by a graduate student. She taught in the English Department of Clackamas Community College from 1991 until her retirement in 2010. She has won an Oregon Literary Arts Fellowship.

Simon Anton Niño Baena spends his spare time on the road with his wife, Xandy. His work has appeared in *Fifth Wednesday Journal, The Cortland Review, San Pedro River Review, Santa Ana River Review, The Bitter Oleander, Catamaran Literary Reader, Cider Press Review, Osiris, Construction Literary Magazine,* and elsewhere.

Chad Bartlett has taught at several schools in Chicago and the San Francisco Bay Area and currently teaches creative writing, literature, and composition at Mt. Hood Community College. His poems have appeared in *Fourteen Hills, The Poet's Voice, Columbia Poetry Review,* and *Sentence,* among others. He shares a home with his girlfriend, daughter, two cats, eight chickens, and three dogs.

Larry Beckett's poetry ranges from songs, Song to the Siren, to blank sonnets, *Songs and Sonnets,* to the epic *American Cycle,* from which *Paul Bunyan* and *Amelia Earhart* have been published, and *Wyatt Earp* is forthcoming. *Beat Poetry* is a study of the poets and poetry of the fifties San Francisco renaissance. He lives in Portland.

Ace Boggess is author of four books of poetry, most recently *I Have Lost the Art of Dreaming It So* (Unsolicited Press, 2018) and *Ultra Deep Field* (Brick Road Poetry Press, 2017), and the novel *A Song Without a Melody* (Hyperborea Publishing, 2016). His writing has appeared in *Harvard Review, Mid-American Review, RATTLE, River Styx, North Dakota Quarterly,* and many other journals. He received a fellowship from the West Virginia Commission on the Arts and spent five years in a West Virginia prison. He lives in Charleston, West Virginia.

Jeffrey S. Chapman is a fiction writer and graphic novelist in the Detroit area. He teaches creative writing at Oakland University. He is working on a graphic novel and his short stories and comics have been published most recently in *The Florida Review, Fiction International,* and *Black Warrior Review.*

Douglas Cole has published five collections of poetry, most recently *The Gold Tooth in the Crooked Smile of God* and a novella, *The Ghost.* His work has appeared and is forthcoming in anthologies and journals such as *The Chicago Quarterly Review, The Atlanta Review, Chiron, Louisiana Literature, The Galway Review, The Coe Review,*

Contributors

and *Slipstream*. He has been nominated for a Pushcart and Best of the Net, and received the Leslie Hunt Memorial Prize in Poetry.

Nick Conrad's poems continue to appear in national and international journals, most recently in *Badlands, Blast Furnace, Blueline, Coe Review, The Comstock Review, The Cortland Review, Fourth River, Hawai'i Pacific Review, Kentucky Review, Mayday Magazine, Orbis* (UK), *Slipstream, Southern Poetry Review, Southword* (Ireland), *Split Rock Review, Stoneboat, Third Wednesday, Valparaiso Poetry Review, West Texas Literary Review,* and *Wilderness House Literary Review*. Work has been accepted for future issues of *Clarion, Common Ground Review, Southern Poetry Review, Stoneboat,* and *The Wayne Literary Review*.

Holly Day's poetry has recently appeared in The Cape Rock, New Ohio Review, and Gargoyle. Her newest poetry collections are A Perfect Day for Semaphore (Finishing Line Press), In This Place, She Is Her Own (Vegetarian Alcoholic Press), A Wall to Protect Your Eyes (Pski's Porch Publishing), I'm in a Place Where Reason Went Missing (Main Street Rag Publishing Co.), and The Yellow Dot of a Daisy (Alien Buddha Press).

Christine DeSimone is a fifth-generation Californian. Her first full-length collection, *How Long the Night Is,* was published by Lummox Press in 2013. Her poems have appeared in *Prairie Schooner, Alaska Quarterly Review, Cream City Review, Cimarron Review, Zyzzyva,* and many other journals. She has also been twice nominated for the Pushcart Prize. She lives in San Francisco with her husband and newborn son.

Contributors

Will Donnelly's work has appeared or is forthcoming in *Barrelhouse, Silk Road, The Potomac Review, Hobart,* and elsewhere, and he is an associate fiction editor at *Juked* magazine. He has an MFA in fiction writing from the Iowa Writers' Workshop and a PhD in literature and creative writing from the University of Houston, and he is an assistant professor of creative writing at Berry College in Rome, Georgia.

Katie Evans likes to draw as a hobby, using mainly pencils or any writing utensil she can find. She only paints when she is in the right environment. She loves learning and has a thirst for knowledge, and hopes to be a famous or at least successful fictional writer. This is her first piece of art to be published. She resides in Oregon City, Oregon, and attends Clackamas Community College.

Nancy Flynn grew up in northeastern Pennsylvania coal country, spent two decades in Ithaca, New York, and now lives in Portland, Oregon. She attended Oberlin College, Cornell University, and has an M.A. in English/Creative Writing from SUNY at Binghamton. Recipient of an Oregon Literary Fellowship, her recent books include *Every Door Recklessly Ajar* and *Great Hunger.*

Taylor Gaede is a freelance writer in South Florida. She has been previously published in *Living Waters Review* and will appear in *Freshwater Literary Journal* and *The Stray Branch.*

Jesse Gardner currently teaches language arts at Madison High School in Portland, OR. Education to him is all about awakening the genius inherent in every person, and one way he likes to awaken genius is through writing poems and raps.

Contributors

Before he settled on a career as an Oregon public school teacher, **Tim Gillespie** worked in warehouses in Los Angeles. Warehouse work—the sweat of cutting open tightly-wrapped boxes and unpacking the contents, working to organize and shelve them in a meaningful way, and then pulling those items back off the shelves to repack and ship off—may have been useful preparation for writing poems and sending them into the world. Gillespie's poems have recently appeared in *Cloudbank*, *Windfall*, *The Timberline Review*, and other places.

LaVonne Griffin-Valade received an MFA in fiction writing from Portland State University in 2017. Her personal essays have been published in *Oregon Humanities Magazine*, and she was a finalist for the 2018 Fellowship for Emerging Writers at Fishtrap's Writing and the West. She has written a novel set in contemporary eastern Oregon and is currently pursuing an agent in hopes of near-future publication.

Suzy Harris lives in Portland, OR. Her poems have appeared in *Calyx*, *Rain*, *VoiceCatcher*, *Windfall*, anthologies produced by the Poetry Box, and an anthology called *Come Shining: Essays and Poems on Writing in a Dark Time*. She has several poems forthcoming in an anthology called *Body Politic: Illustrated poems about the body and disability*.

Marie Hartung writes from her living room recliner in the smallish town of Monroe, WA. She's a double-concentration graduate in poetry and nonfiction, from the Whidbey Island Writers' Workshop MFA program and works as a Realtor, HR Consultant, and Freelance Writer. Her poetry and nonfiction work has appeared in *Slab*, *East Jasmine Review*, *Talking River*, *Poetry Quarterly*, *Thin Air*, *Whidbey*

Life Magazine, Soundings Review, Third Wednesday, Cordite Review, Perceptions Literary Magazine, River Poets Journal, Raven Chronicles, and in the anthology *The Burden of Light*. She was named a 2014 finalist for the Writers at Work Fellowship, 2014 finalist for the Eric Hoffer Award for Prose and a recipient of a fellowship scholarship award for the Summer Literary Series in Kenya. She has two sons age 10 and 13 who are the love of her life, although, NY pizza is a close second.

Madronna Holden is a folklorist and storyteller whose award-winning poetry has appeared in the anthology, *Dona Nobis Pacem*, as well as in journals such as *American Writing, Northwest Magazine, The Christian Science Monitor, Fireweed, Windfall, the Aurorean, Leaping Clear, Cathexis NW*, and is forthcoming in *Equinox* and *The New Southerner*, among others. The community production of her full-length poetry drama, *The Descent of Inanna*, was the subject of a special aired on Oregon Public Broadcasting. She is taking the opportunity of her recent retirement from university teaching to concentrate on her poetry, including a book of poems, *Going the Distance*, written in response to watercolors painted by David Wolfersberger on his 3500 miles bicycle tour of the West Coast.

James Croal Jackson has a chapbook, *The Frayed Edge of Memory* (Writing Knights Press, 2017), and poems in *Columbia Journal, Rattle*, and *Reservoir*. He edits *The Mantle*. Currently, he works in the film industry in Pittsburgh, PA.

John P. Kristofco has published seven hundred poems and sixty short stories in about two hundred different publications, including: *Folio,*

Contributors

Rattle, Bryant Literary Review, Cimarron Review, Fourth River, Stand, The MacGuffin, Sierra Nevada Review, Blueline, Slant, Snowy Egret, and *Clackamas Literary Review*. He has published four collections of poetry, most recently *The Timekeeper's Garden* from The Orchard Street Press, and is currently putting together a book of short stories. Jack has been nominated for the Pushcart Prize five times. He lives in Highland Heights, Ohio, with his wife Kathy.

David Mihalyov lives outside of Rochester, NY, with his wife, two daughters, and two dogs. His writing has appeared in several journals, including in *Concho River Review, Gravel, New Plains Review, San Pedro River Review,* and *Timberline Review*.

Cecil Morris retired after 37 years of teaching English—mostly at Roseville High School in Roseville, California. Now he tries writing himself what he spent so many years teaching others to understand and enjoy. In his newly abundant spare time, he has been reading Sharon Olds, Megan Peak, Naomi Shihab Nye, and Morgan Parker. He enjoys ice cream too much and cruciferous vegetables too little. He has had a handful of poems published in *English Journal, The Ekphrastic Review, Poem, Dime Show Review, The American Scholar,* and other literary magazines.

Linda Neal lives with her dog, Mantra, near the beach. She studied literature at Pomona College, earned a degree in linguistics and a master's degree in clinical psychology. Her poems and essays have appeared in, or are forthcoming, in numerous journals, including *Crack the Spine, Landlocked* (formerly Beecher's), *Lummox, Peregrine, Prairie Schooner, Santa Fe Literary Review,* and *SLAB* and have won awards from

Beyond Baroque Foundation, *Pacific Coast Journal*, PEN Women Writers, and San Luis Obispo Golden Quill. *Dodge & Burn*, her first collection (Bambaz Press) came out in 2014. She is enrolled in Pacific University's MFA program in poetry and is working on her second collection.

Daniel J. Nickolas has long been fascinated with language and storytelling, and believes that there is no such thing as a true synonym. He has previously published with *Pathos Literary Magazine* and *The Pacific Sentinel*. His favorite storytellers include John Steinbeck, Franz Kafka, and all the German grandmothers who kept fairytales alive, before the Brothers Grimm wrote those tales down. Daniel currently works as the German tutor at Portland State University.

Francis Opila has lived in the Pacific Northwest most of his adult life; he currently resides in Portland, OR. His work, recreation, and spirit have taken him out into the woods, wetlands, mountains, and rivers. He works as an environmental scientist, primarily with water quality. His poems have appeared in *Parks and Points*, *Windfall*, *Soul-Lit*, among others. He enjoys performing poetry, combining recitation and playing Native American flute.

Ty Phelps is a writer, teacher, and musician. He won *The Gravity of the Thing's* 2016 Six Word Story Contest, and was a finalist for *Gigantic Sequins* flash fiction contest that same year. His work has been printed in *Writespace*, *1001 Journal*, and *Scribble*, among others. He lives in Madison, WI, where he teaches high school English, plays drums, enjoys decaf coffee. He is currently teaching himself to play the banjo.

Contributors

Corey S. Pressman is an imagination professional who works with organizations and individuals to incorporate the arts & humanities, intentional mind wandering, and collective ideation into their creative practice. He has published poetry, short stories, and academic works.

Will Radke is from Oak Park, IL. His fiction has appeared in *Typehouse Literary Magazine*, *Avalon Literary Review*, *Hypertext Magazine*, and elsewhere.

Susan Bruns Rowe writes and teaches in Boise, Idaho. Her work has appeared or is forthcoming in *Brevity*, *Creative Nonfiction*, *The Louisville Review*, and elsewhere. She serves on the editorial staff for *Literary Mama* and teaches creative writing for two nonprofits. She recently completed a manuscript of short stories based on the lives of her immigrant grandparents.

Mark Rubin has published one book of poems, *The Beginning of Responsibility* (Owl Creek Press). His work has appeared in *The Gettysburg Review*, *The Ohio Review*, *Prairie Schooner*, *The Virginia Quarterly Review*, *The Yale Review*, and elsewhere. A past recipient of the Discovery/The Nation Award and a National Endowment for the Arts Fellowship, he lives in Burlington, VT, where he is a psychotherapist in private practice.

Peter Serchuk's poems have appeared in a variety of journals including *Boulevard*, *Denver Quarterly*, *Hudson Review*, *North American Review*, *Texas Review*, *Atlanta Rebiew*, *New Plains Review*, and others. He is the author of *Waiting for Poppa at the Smithtown Diner* (University of Illinois Press) and *All That Remains* (WordTech Editions). A new collection of short poems, *The Purpose of Things* (with photographs by Pieter de Koninck), is forthcoming from Regal House Publishing in 2019. He lives in Carmel, CA.

Tara K. Shepersky is a taxonomist, poet, essayist, and photographer, based in the Willamette Valley. Her creative work explores the ways our inner and outer, individual and collective experiences listen, speak, and shape themselves to the land we live beside. Recent work has appeared in *Shark Reef*, *Cascadia Rising Review*, *Sky Island Journal*, *Mojave Heart Review*, and *Empty Mirror*, among others.

Ben Slotky is the author of *Red Hot Dogs, White Gravy* (Chiasmus, 2010/Widow & Orphan, 2017) and *An Evening of Romantic Lovemaking* (Dalkey Archive, 2021). His work has appeared in *The Santa Monica Review*, *Numero Cinq*, *The Forge*, *Hobart*, *Golden Handcuffs Review*, *Barrelhouse*, *Juked*, and many other publications. He lives in Bloomington, IL, with his wife and six sons.

Matthew J. Spireng's book *What Focus Is* was published in 2011 by WordTech Communications. His book *Out of Body* won the 2004 Bluestem Poetry Award and was published in 2006 by Bluestem Press at Emporia State University. He won The MacGuffin's 23rd Annual Poet Hunt, judged by Alberto Rios, and is an eight-time Pushcart Prize nominee.

Hollyn Taylor is a lifelong misfit and a writer of fiction. She is a former assistant editor of the *Clackamas Literary Review* and studied creative writing at Clackamas Community College. She lives in Southern Oregon with her friends and a herd of cats.

Contributors

Chelsea Thiel is a former student of Clackamas Community College and a current student at Prescott College where she is pursuing a Bachelor's degree in English. She wrote "Conflagration of the Heart," a one-act play that was produced and performed in the student showcase at Clackamas Community College.

Evan Morgan Williams is the author of two collections of stories: *Thorn*, winner of the 2013 Chandra Prize (BkMk Press, University of Missouri-Kansas City), and *Canyons* (printed privately, 2018). Williams' stories have appeared in such magazines as *Witness*, *Antioch Review*, *Kenyon Review*, and *Alaska Quarterly Review*. He holds an MFA from the University of Montana, and he has taught in our public schools for 27 years. A two-time mentor in AWP's Writer2Writer program, Williams is currently at work on a novel, a literary noir set in—where else—Los Angeles.

John Sibley Williams is the author of *As One Fire Consumes Another* (Orison Poetry Prize, 2019), *Skin Memory* (Backwaters Prize, 2019), *Disinheritance*, and *Controlled Hallucinations*. A nineteen-time Pushcart nominee, John is the winner of numerous awards, including the Philip Booth Award, American Literary Review Poetry Contest, Phyllis Smart-Young Prize, The 46er Prize, Nancy D. Hargrove Editors' Prize, Confrontation Poetry Prize, and Laux/Millar Prize. He serves as editor of *The Inflectionist Review* and works as a literary agent. Previous publishing credits include: *The Yale Review*, *Midwest Quarterly*, *Southern Review*, *Sycamore Review*, *Prairie Schooner*, *The Massachusetts Review*, *Poet Lore*, *Saranac Review*, *Atlanta Review*, *TriQuarterly*, *Columbia Poetry Review*, *Mid-American Review*, *Poetry Northwest*, *Third Coast*, and various anthologies. He lives in Portland, Oregon.

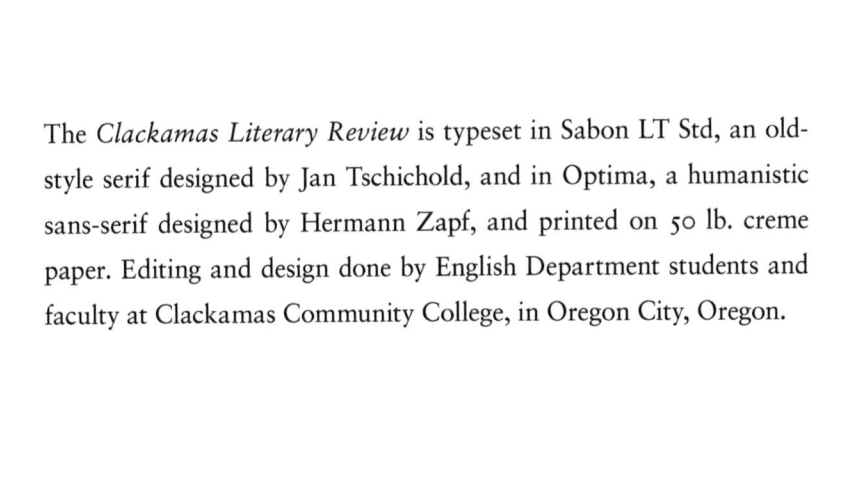

The *Clackamas Literary Review* is typeset in Sabon LT Std, an old-style serif designed by Jan Tschichold, and in Optima, a humanistic sans-serif designed by Hermann Zapf, and printed on 50 lb. creme paper. Editing and design done by English Department students and faculty at Clackamas Community College, in Oregon City, Oregon.

Visit

CLR
CLACKAMAS LITERARY REVIEW

clackamasliteraryreview.org
clackamasliteraryreview.submittable.com
facebook.com/clackamasliteraryreview
@clackamaslitrev

Contact
clr@clackamas.edu

CLR
CLACKAMAS LITERARY REVIEW

the finest writing for the best readers

Clackamas Literary Review has been committed to publishing quality writing from around the world since 1997. Use the form below or visit us on Submittable to receive the latest and forthcoming issues.

Clackamas Literary Review

_____ 1 year $12

_____ 2 years $22

_____ 3 years $32

Name _____

Address _____

City / State / Zip _____

Email _____

Send this form and check or money order to:

Clackamas Literary Review
English Department
Clackamas Community College
19600 Molalla Avenue
Oregon City, Oregon 97045

CPSIA information can be obtained
at www.ICGtesting.com
Printed in the USA
FFHW02195418051 9
525418 53-579 93FF